TROUBLE
AT
WILD RIVER

Adventures
of the Northwoods

TROUBLE
AT
WILD RIVER

Lois Walfrid Johnson

BETHANY HOUSE PUBLISHERS
MINNEAPOLIS, MINNESOTA 55438

Big Gust Anderson, Gust Berglund, Walfrid and Edla Johnson, John Peterson, Steven and Edith Powell, and Charles and Hannah Saunders lived in the Grantsburg/St. Croix River area during the early 1900s. Except for the location of the maple trees tapped, Katherine Cloud is based on the historic Katherine Cloud who lived on the Trade River. All other characters in this book are fictitious. Any resemblance to persons living or dead is coincidental. The geographic locations are accurate with the exception of Sand Creek, which is fictitious.

Cover illustration by Andrea Jorgenson.

Published by Bethany House Publishers
A Ministry of Bethany Fellowship, Inc.
6820 Auto Club Road, Minneapolis, Minnesota 55438

Printed in the United States of America

Library of Congress Cataloging-in-Publication Data

Johnson, Lois Walfrid.
    Trouble at Wild River / Lois W. Johnson.
        p. cm. — (The Adventures of the northwoods ; bk. 5)
    Summary: In 1907 in Wisconsin, Kate and her friends discover a timber swindler while visiting their Indian friend Joe and suspect that Kate's uncle, newly arrived from Sweden, may be involved.

    [1. Swedish Americans—Fiction.   2. Logging—Fiction. 3. Wisconsin—Fiction. 4. Uncles—Fiction. 5. Indians of North America—Fiction. 6. Christian life—Fiction. 7. Mystery and detective stories.] I. Title. II. Series: Johnson, Lois Walfrid. Adventures of the northwoods ; bk. 5.
PZ7.J63255Tr 1991
[Fic]—dc20
ISBN 1–55661–144–7

91–26802
CIP
AC

To Jeff and Cynthia
Daniel and Justin

with my love and appreciation
for the way you are.

LOIS WALFRID JOHNSON is the author of over twenty books, including *You're Worth More Than You Think* and other books in the Let's-Talk-About-It Stories for Kids Series to help preteens make wise choices. Novels in the Adventures of the Northwoods Series have received awards from Excellence in Media, the Wisconsin State Historical Society, and the Council for Wisconsin Writers.

Lois and her husband, Roy, who plays a supportive role in her writing, are the parents of three married children and live in rural Wisconsin.

In the time in which this book was set the Native Americans in the St. Croix Band of northwest Wisconsin were called Chippewa. In recent years many are once again using the name of Ojibwa (Oh-JIB-wah).

Contents

1

Mysterious Noises

*I*n the glow of the lantern Katherine O'Connell's deep blue eyes sparkled. As she brushed aside the black hair escaping her braid, she looked ahead. Wildfire, the mare, trotted easily over the patches of snow, pulling the farm wagon in which Kate rode.

Far above, a lopsided moon lit the sky. On that cloudless March night the stars shone brightly, seeming just beyond the treetops. Sitting between her stepbrother Anders and her friend Erik Lundgren, Kate felt warm and safe.

Then, as Anders turned Wildfire onto a trail through the woods, an owl hooted. From off in the distance the call came— each note a lonesome cry. Kate shivered, but not from cold.

As the mare stretched out her legs, long shadows fell across the path. Like pointing fingers, pine branches reached toward the wagon, almost touching Kate.

Soon the call came again. *Whoo, whoo, whoo, whoo—whoo, whoo, whoo, whoo-ah!*

"That's not an owl," said Erik in the quiet that followed.

"It isn't?" asked Kate. "Then what is it?"

"Someone signaling." The lantern Erik held cast a flickering light on his wavy brown hair. But certainty filled his eyes. "Shhhhh!"

Anders reined in the mare, and the hooting seemed closer this time.

"It's a barred owl," Anders said as the call faded away.

"No, it's not." Erik sounded sure of himself. "It's someone talking through the woods."

Anders laughed. "I thought Kate was the one with a big imagination."

"She is," said Erik. "This isn't imagination. It's real."

"Yah, sure," Anders told him. "You betcha." He flicked the reins across Wildfire's back, and the mare stepped out.

But Kate felt curious. "Erik, how do you know? Why do you think it's not an owl?"

"I can't explain it," he answered. "I just hear the difference."

As Wildfire trotted on, Kate stared into the darkness, hoping to catch a glimpse of a large owl. Yet she knew Erik was seldom wrong. His ability in music helped him recognize other sounds as well.

"If it's not an owl, what is it?" Kate asked.

"You mean *who* is it," said Anders. "*Who* is creeping around in the depths of night? *Who* is ready to snatch you from this wagon?"

"Oh, Anders!" Since coming to northwest Wisconsin, Kate had fought against her fear of the nighttime woods. Yet she didn't want to admit that fear to this stepbrother who was also thirteen. Like Erik, Anders was six feet tall and broad-shouldered from farm work.

Pretending she wasn't afraid, Kate gazed up into branches still without leaves from winter. No large owl flew from tree to tree.

In that March of 1907, the northwest Wisconsin days had been warm. Yet the nights dropped below freezing, providing perfect weather for a strong flow of sap from the sugar maples. For two weeks farmers and their families had worked hard, collecting the thin sap and boiling it down.

Dark came early to these woods, and Kate felt concerned that she'd miss what she wanted to see. "You're sure Joe's grand-mother will still be making syrup?" Kate looked forward to meeting the Chippewa family.

"Yup," Anders told her. "He said his grandma would work late. She'll be finishing up for the day."

Joe's grandparents owned a farm on Trade River. Anders and Erik had known the Indian boy for some time, but Kate was new to the area. A year before, her mother had married Anders' father, and Mama and Kate moved from Minneapolis to Windy Hill Farm.

"Why does the Cloud family use trees near here?" Kate asked.

"They don't have sugar maples on their own land," Erik told her. "Usually they tap trees closer to home. This year Mrs. Cloud asked a farmer near Big Wood Lake if she could use his maples. When she gets done, she'll give him syrup and candy."

A grin crossed her brother's face. "You know, Kate, you can help Joe with all the work. That is, if you can keep up to him."

By now Kate knew Anders well enough to see through most of his teasing. Still she was curious. "What does he do?"

"Gathers wood to keep the fire going. Collects pails filled with sap. Brings 'em in to the fire."

"It's hard work," said Erik. "Joe's brothers help too. They start when the sap begins running in the morning and keep on till it slows down at night."

As Anders turned the mare into the ruts of yet another trail, Kate asked, "Where are you going?"

Anders flicked the reins. "Taking a shortcut along the lake."

"With all the warm weather, it might be mucky in there," Erik warned.

Anders acted as if he didn't hear. Before long, the trees on either side of the path thinned out.

Again Wildfire slowed her pace and stepped gingerly. Suddenly she sank knee-deep into mud.

Nervously the mare tossed her head. Anders clucked to her.

"You're all right," Anders called, his voice soothing. "C'mon, girl. Giddyup!"

Wildfire turned her ears to the sound of his voice and lunged into the harness. The wagon jerked forward as the wheels churned through the mud.

As they moved more and more slowly, Kate grew impatient. "We'll be too late!" she said to Anders.

Her tall, blond brother paid no attention. At last they came to an open area with no trees. Here and there patches of snow remained on the ice of Big Wood Lake.

A large black heap loomed up in the darkness. Soon Kate saw more dark shapes along the shore. As they drew closer, she realized what they were—great piles of neatly stacked logs.

During the winter, farmers around the lake worked hard, cutting trees on their land. By selling the logs to a large company, the men earned money they needed for their families.

"When the ice goes out, the farmers will open the dam," Erik said. He pointed into the darkness. "The logs will go out of Big Wood Lake, through the dam, and down the Wood River to the St. Croix."*

Kate knew that the St. Croix River marked the border between Wisconsin and Minnesota. Once there, the logs floated downstream to sawmills at Stillwater, Minnesota.

Just then Anders stopped the mare, turned his head, and listened.

Quickly Erik blew out the flame of the lantern. "Shhhhh!" he warned.

Anders slipped to the ground and slogged forward in the mud. Standing by Wildfire's head, he laid his hand on her neck.

A moment later Kate heard what she'd missed before. From a short distance away came a strange sound. What was it?

When Erik dropped down, she knew he'd heard the same thing. Kate followed him, leaping over the mud in the track to walk on firmer ground near the trees.

Soon she caught up to her brother. He stood still, as though

---

*The river that divides Minnesota and Wisconsin is pronounced "Saint *Kroy*."

listening. When Wildfire moved restlessly, Anders laid his fingers across the mare's muzzle.

In the stillness Kate heard the mysterious noise again.

Wildfire stomped her foot. Anders quieted her, then led her off the path. In the light of the moon Kate saw him tie the mare's lead rope to a tree. Lowering her head, Wildfire began eating the brown grass that reached through the little snow that remained.

When Anders returned to them, Erik took the lead. By now Kate felt curious. What was going on? Why were the boys being so careful? She felt afraid to speak, even in a whisper.

Erik reached the first pile of logs and waited until Kate and Anders caught up. Though the boys were six feet tall, the logs towered above them. From somewhere beyond, the sound came clearly.

Then Erik moved on, a shadow darker than those around him. As Kate and Anders followed, the soft ground deadened their footsteps. When they reached the next pile of logs, they again stopped to listen.

This time Kate recognized the sound of sawing wood. But why would anyone work in the dark? What was he trying to hide?

Pushing aside her uneasiness, Kate followed Erik to the third pile of logs. This one was smaller. In spite of her short height, Kate looked over it.

Not far away, a lantern sat on the ground. The light of its flame reflected on a nearby saw.

A man dressed in dark clothes crouched close to still another pile of logs. He worked quickly, filling a gunnysack with slices of wood from the ground.

When the sack bulged, the man closed and tied it. Then he picked up a tool with a wooden handle. *What is it?* Kate wondered. *An ax?*

As the man moved closer to the lantern, Kate had a better look at the tool he was using. It seemed different from an ax— more like a small sledgehammer.

Taking a stand near the end of the logs, he swung the hammer. In the crisp night air, iron thudded against wood. Again and again the man swung, striking the end of one log after another.

After a time he straightened up. Turning his head, he seemed to listen. In that instant Wildfire whinnied.

The man leaped over to the lantern and blew out the flame. In the darkness running footsteps were heard. Then all was quiet.

Kate blinked, struggling to see beyond the small flame that danced before her eyes. Anders darted forward, and she followed.

Erik took one way, Kate another, and Anders a third, searching as quickly as they could without a light. Yet they found no dark shape kneeling down, trying to hide within the shelter of the logs. Whoever had been there was gone.

Then Kate heard a noise farther off. "Over there!" she called.

As she ran in that direction, she rounded a great pile of logs. One log stuck out farther than the others and caught her in the chest. Kate's arms flew up, and she fell backward into the darkness of night.

2

The Timber Swindler

The next instant Kate landed hard. *I can't breathe*, she thought. *I can't catch my breath.*

For what seemed an eternity she lay still, too stunned to move. Then Erik called, "Kate, where are you?"

She heard his voice, but could not respond.

Erik kneeled down, close to her head. "What happened? Are you hurt?"

But Kate couldn't answer.

"Knocked the wind out of her," Anders said.

Kate groaned and finally drew a long, ragged breath. From a short distance away she heard a quick movement. Was the man escaping?

Then Kate felt the dampness of the ground on which she lay. The cold crept through her long stockings and dress.

Turning her head, she opened her eyes. In the light of the moon she saw how scared Erik and Anders looked.

Erik helped her sit up.

"What were you doing?" demanded Anders. "Don't you know that's a good way to get hurt?"

Kate flinched at the sound of her brother's voice. It made no difference that he always talked that way when he was upset. Listening to him, Kate felt even worse.

"I got hurt all right," she muttered when she could speak.

"I mean *really* hurt," Anders grumbled. "What were you thinking, running after that man? What if he decided to go after *you*?"

She hadn't been thinking, Kate knew that. She just wanted to make sure the man didn't get away. Yet she didn't care to admit her mistake to Anders.

Slowly she stood up. Bending over, she tried to brush the dirt off her coat and long stockings.

As she wavered, Erik caught her hand. "Be quiet, Anders," he said. "She knows it was a dumb move."

"Dumb, was it?" Kate was returning to normal. She dropped Erik's hand, wanting no more of his help.

Anders hurried to the wagon and returned with the farm lantern. Erik lit it again, and the two boys searched the area. After studying the ends of the logs, they walked in a circle, holding out the light.

Soon the lantern bobbed away. Kate started to follow, then realized she still felt shaken from the jarring she'd taken.

As the light disappeared, Kate trembled. Were the boys finding footprints in the soft ground? She didn't like being all alone. What if the man came back?

When the minutes stretched long, Kate returned to the wagon and climbed up to the high spring seat. Looking about, she gazed up at the night sky and the lopsided moon. Right now she'd welcome an owl with its large feathery body passing between the tall trees.

A cold wind blew from the lake, and she huddled beneath a blanket. From somewhere behind, a branch snapped. Kate jumped.

She twisted around, and the glow of a lantern pierced the darkness. Two dark shapes separated from the trees. When Anders and Erik stepped out, Kate felt relieved.

"We followed quite a ways," Erik told her. "But we lost him when the ground got firm."

The two boys climbed into the wagon, and Anders clucked to Wildfire. As they started off once more, he looked down at Kate. "Because of you, that man got away."

"Because of *me!*" Kate exclaimed. Sitting up, she flipped her long braid over her shoulder. "Because of Wildfire, you mean. She whinnied."

"If you hadn't landed flat on your face, we could have kept up with him," Anders said.

It was true, Kate knew, and she probably felt sorrier than anyone. Already she felt better and as curious as usual. "What was that man doing?"

"Stealing logs," Anders growled.

"Stealing logs? How do you know?"

"Remember the sawing we heard?" Erik asked. "The man was cutting thin slices off the end of each log. Looked like he had a gunnysack—"

"For picking up the slices," Kate said. Until now, she hadn't understood all that was happening. She knew only that whatever the man was doing, it had to be wrong. He was trying too hard to keep it a secret.

"Why did he hit the logs with a sledgehammer?" she asked.

"It wasn't a sledge." Anders urged Wildfire ahead. Here the trail was firmer, and the mare moved faster.

"It's a smaller hammer," said Erik. "It's smaller and lighter and called a stamp hammer. On both sides of the iron head there's a raised design that makes a mark."

"Like the brand ranchers use on cattle?"

"Sort of. But ranchers use a hot iron to mark an animal's hide. Loggers pound their mark on the end of a log."

As the boys talked, Kate learned that every farmer who sent logs down the river, as well as every logging company, had their own special mark. In the light of the lantern she saw Erik's eyes.

"Loggers get paid according to how many logs come in with their mark," he explained.

"So the man is a timber swindler," Kate said slowly. "He pretends something that isn't his belongs to him."

Erik nodded. "And the farmers who work hard cutting down

trees won't get paid for their logs. It's the same as stealing money from them."

Kate breathed deeply, and knew she was back to normal. At the same time, just thinking about the swindler made her afraid. What would he try to do next?

Before long, Erik leaped down from the wagon to open a gate. In the pasture through which they passed, the woods thinned out. A fire glowed in the darkness.

As they drew closer, Kate saw four upright poles at the corners of the fire. Between them stretched other poles that crossed above the flames. From this framework a number of chains hung down. One held a huge iron kettle. Other chains held smaller kettles and pails.

An Indian woman wearing a long dress stirred the contents of the largest kettle. When Anders stopped Wildfire, a slender youth of about fourteen came forward.

"Joe, meet Kate," Anders said.

In the light of the lantern the boy grinned. With black hair and dancing black eyes, he looked athletic and strong.

"C'mon with us," Anders told him. As Wildfire trotted through the pasture into the farmyard, Joe ran next to the wagon.

At the hitching rail Kate climbed down and started for the house. Erik stayed close by and made sure she felt all right.

When Anders knocked, young children opened the door and went to find their father.

"Come in," the man said. "We're just having coffee."

In the warm kitchen, Kate saw another man and two women at the round table. As they looked her way, they stopped talking.

Then Kate saw beyond them. A tall man stood along the wall. His head reached more than a foot above the doorway.

"Big Gust!" Kate exclaimed. She was surprised to see the seven-foot, six-inch-tall Swede. "I forgot that your sister lives near here."

As marshall in the nearby village of Grantsburg, Big Gust had helped Kate and Anders solve a mystery more than once. Now a welcome grin lit the giant's face.

"God dag, god dag," he said. It sounded like "Good dog," but Kate knew it was the Swedish hello.

Then Big Gust glanced beyond her to the boys, and his smile faded. Quickly he moved around the table. "What's wrong?" he asked.

For the first time Kate realized how she looked. Small pieces of wood clung to her coat. Here and there smudges of dirt darkened the cloth, as well as her stockings and dress. She stepped back, wishing she could hide.

But Big Gust was already following the boys outside. As Kate joined them, Anders spoke quickly, telling the marshall what had happened.

Big Gust wasted no time. His deep voice rumbled as he said, "Just a minute." When he returned from the house, he wore his coat and brought the two men. The marshall towered over both of them.

Kate and the boys hurried toward Wildfire. As Kate climbed up and sat down on the high seat, Anders spoke sharply. "You're not going with us."

"Yes, I am," answered Kate.

"No, you're not," said her brother.

Then Erik came alongside, and Kate turned to him. "I can go, can't I?"

Erik shook his head. "It's not safe."

Kate couldn't believe what she was hearing. "I was in on the beginning. Why can't I go now?"

Anders climbed up beside her. "This is just for men."

"For men!" Kate sputtered. "You and Erik aren't men!"

"Yah, but we are!" Raising one arm, Anders flexed his muscles.

"We're in a hurry, Kate," said Erik as he waited for her to get down.

Kate glanced toward Joe, who stood a short way off. She felt embarrassed at being treated like a baby. "Why can't I go?" she asked her brother.

"Because you might get hurt again." Erik looked at her steadily.

Knowing that she had no choice, Kate climbed down. She started for the house with her back stiff and straight. Yet when she heard Anders cluck to Wildfire, her curiosity proved too much.

Kate looked around to see the spirited black horse take the lead. Another wagon with Big Gust and the two men followed.

Then Joe bounded across the yard. His feet were swift and light and skimmed the patches of snow. As Anders entered the trail into the woods, the boy caught up and ran alongside.

He runs as swift as a deer, Kate thought as she watched Joe. Already she understood why Anders and Erik liked him.

Then the wagons disappeared from sight. Again Kate longed to be with them, to see what was happening. Had the timber swindler returned to the logs? Or was he, even now, hiding somewhere among the trees?

3

Kate Decides

*T*rying to push aside her disappointment, Kate followed the trail the wagons had taken out of the farmyard. With each step she wondered where the swindler was now. Then she wondered about the men and boys. *Are they headed into danger?*

Walking quickly through the pasture, Kate soon saw flames leaping upward in the darkness. In spite of everything that had happened, she felt excited about watching Joe's family make syrup.

When she reached the fire, she found children of all sizes gathered around Joe's grandmother. Eagerly they waited for the syrup to boil down into candy.

As Kate watched, Mrs. Cloud took smaller pails from chains hanging above the sides of the fire. From these she poured sap into the large black kettle hanging over the center.

Erik had told Kate it took more than thirty pails of sap—perhaps even forty—to make one pail of syrup. But that was all she knew.

"How do you get sap from the trees?" Kate asked Mrs. Cloud.

The grandmother looked her way without speaking. Yet Kate felt sure that she heard.

Kate opened her mouth to speak again and just as quickly closed it. As though it were yesterday, she remembered her first day at Spirit Lake School. She'd been the only one unable to speak Swedish. Now she wondered, *Does Mrs. Cloud speak a language I don't understand?* Kate wished she knew the words to use.

"I'm Katherine O'Connell," she said finally.

Mrs. Cloud pointed to herself. "Katherine."

Kate felt confused. "Katherine O'Connell," she repeated, pointing to her own self.

The grandmother broke into a smile. "Katherine Cloud," she said.

"Really?" Kate asked. "*You're* Katherine too?"

Her eyes sparkling with laughter, Mrs. Cloud nodded.

Just then a boy of nine or ten brought in wood for the fire. A younger boy carried pails filled with sap. As Kate watched, he emptied the sap into a large stock tank.

Mrs. Cloud spoke to the older of the two boys, using another language. When the grandmother finished speaking, the boy turned to Kate.

"Mamana speaks Chippewa," he said in English.

"*Mamana?*" Kate asked. It was a new word for her.

"It means *my mother*," he explained. "Our mother calls our grandmother that, and so do we. What do you want?"

Again Kate wished she knew the language. She felt grateful someone could translate. "I want to know how she makes maple syrup and candy."

Turning back to Mamana, he spoke rapidly. When Mrs. Cloud glanced toward the woods, the boy gave Kate a couple of pails and took one for himself. Carrying a farm lantern, he headed for the trees.

"Who are you?" Kate asked, as she followed him.

"I'm Peter," he said. Though shorter than Kate, he seemed taller because of the way he carried himself.

Soon they reached the sugar maples. Holding out the lantern, Peter explained how they cut a diagonal slit in each tree from which they collected sap. They inserted a small narrow trough just below the newly made opening.

The sap had stopped dripping for the night, but Kate saw a clear thin liquid in the birchbark container below the wooden trough.

Peter explained that not everyone tapped trees in this way. Some families pushed out the soft center of a sumac branch to use a tube instead of a trough.

The boy went from tree to tree. Each time he found a full container, he poured the sap into one of the pails they carried.

"You're Joe's brother?" Kate asked, as they started back to the others.

When Peter nodded, his eyes glowed with pride. "Joe runs miles without stopping."

"Miles?" asked Kate, curious how far Joe could go.

"Many, many miles," Peter said. "He runs faster than anyone I know."

Kate was sure that Peter's pride was more than a young boy bragging about his older brother. "Are you a good runner too?" she asked.

"Not as fast as Joe," Peter answered. "But I will be."

For the rest of the way, he told her everything he knew about his big brother. As she listened to Peter, Kate wondered what had happened to Joe and Erik and Anders. Why were they taking so long?

When Kate and Peter reached the fire, they emptied the sap they carried into the large stock tank. Then they joined the children gathered around Mrs. Cloud.

Before long the grandmother strained the syrup she had cooked down and filled several large containers. Using a long paddle, she continued stirring the contents of the biggest kettle. When the syrup thickened even more, the moment the children had been waiting for arrived.

With a wooden ladle, Mrs. Cloud poured some of the thick syrup into small containers. She poured other syrup into a clean patch of snow. Soon the snow hardened the syrup into candy.

The minute it was cool enough to eat, Peter gave Kate a piece. As her mouth closed around the maple candy, she wondered if she had ever tasted anything so delicious.

When she finished eating, Kate walked over to the woman who still worked by the fire. "Mrs. Cloud," she said. "Mrs. *Katherine* Cloud."

A glint of laughter lit the grandmother's eyes.

"The candy is very good," said Kate, and she was sure Mamana understood.

By the time the wagons returned, it was late. "We'll post a watch every night," Kate heard one of the men say to Big Gust.

"Hop in!" Anders told Kate.

"What happened?" she asked, as they headed back over the trail.

"Nothing." Anders sounded tired and discouraged.

"What do you mean?"

"We stopped quite a ways off and left the horses. But there must have been a bear around—"

"A bear?" When Kate lived in Minneapolis her friend Sarah Livingston told her there would be bears in these woods. Ever since moving to northwest Wisconsin, Kate had expected to see one.

"Whatever it was, it spooked the horses," Anders said. "One of the men stayed with them, but right after we left, Wildfire started thrashing around. She snorted and made all kinds of noises. I ran back to her, but it was too late."

"Too late for what?"

Anders sighed. "If the timber swindler came back, he sure wasn't around when we got there. He had plenty of time to clean up anything we missed."

"Whoever the man is, he's mighty tricky," said Erik. "And dangerous."

"Did the owl hoot again?" Kate asked.

"Yup," Erik told her. "But this time it was real."

"Oh, Erik! Are you sure you can tell the difference?"

"I'm sure," Erik said quietly. "Even Anders agreed with me."

When they pulled into the Windy Hill farmyard, the boys worked together to unhitch Wildfire.

As Anders headed toward the barn, Kate spoke softly, hoping

he wouldn't hear. "I'm sorry, Erik. I'm sorry that the swindler got away because of me."

"That's all right," he said. "Any one of us could have fallen."

Anders turned back. "We could have, but we didn't."

A surge of anger rushed through Kate. Flipping her long braid over her shoulder, she hurried off. By the time she reached the kitchen door, she'd made up her mind. From now on, she'd do her best not to be left out of anything. From now on, she'd prove to Anders she could keep up with him or any other boy.

At breakfast the next morning Kate and Anders told the Nordstrom family about the timber swindler. As they sat around the kitchen table, they spoke in English. Yet five-year-old Tina, who had not yet learned English in school, seemed to understand. With white-blond hair wisping around her face, she looked from Kate to Anders, her blue eyes wide.

Nine-year-old Lars listened to every word without speaking. As usual, a tuft of red hair stood up at the back of his head. Beneath his freckles, he still looked pale from his bout with pneumonia.

Except for a question now and then, Mama remained silent. Even this early in the day, she had combed her golden hair upward, piling it on top of her head.

Mama's pretty, thought Kate. Her mother moved slowly these days. Beneath Mama's large apron and the blue dress that matched her eyes, the baby she expected had grown large.

As Anders talked, Kate watched her mother. Though it had been just a year ago, it seemed a long time since she and Mama lived in Minneapolis. It was even longer since Daddy O'Connell died in a construction accident. But Kate remembered those days well. She remembered how often she woke up to hear Mama crying in the night.

Now whenever Mama looked at Papa Nordstrom, her eyes seemed to glow. Even her smile looked soft.

When Anders finished talking, Papa had the most questions.

With a frown on his bearded face, he asked Anders to go back over the details.

"You actually saw the man cut off an end from each log?"

"We couldn't see that, but we heard it," Anders said. "We watched him put thin slices of wood into a sack. We think he stirred the dirt around, because we couldn't find sawdust."

"And there was a new mark on the end of the logs?"

"You betcha," said Anders. "When we went back, Big Gust and the other men checked the mark. None of the farmers who log around there use the one we saw."

"Well, I suppose the first thing to do is to warn the mill people at Stillwater. Find out who registered the false end mark."

"Big Gust said the same thing. He'll talk to Charlie Saunders."

"The county sheriff?" asked Mama.

Anders nodded. "Charlie will talk to someone at the mill. But Big Gust knew it might not do a bit of good. The swindler probably gave a false name. And now he knows we've seen what he's doing. If he's smart, he'll change the mark he uses."

Papa sighed. "Farmers are going to lose a lot of money if the thief isn't caught—money they really need. What's more, I don't like having a timber swindler wandering around the woods."

"We'll stay close to the house, Carl," Mama quickly assured him. "And before long the little one will come."

Papa smiled, and the frown on his face disappeared. "Yah. Soon we'll have another Nordstrom."

Tina looked at Mama and spoke quickly in Swedish. Kate understood Tina's question: "Do you think it'll be a boy or a girl?"

Mama's gentle smile erased the tired lines around her eyes. "We'll take whatever God gives us. And we'll be thankful."

"Are you hoping for a girl?" Lars asked Kate.

"For sure," she answered. "No more brothers!"

But Anders broke in. "No more *sisters*, you mean!"

"No more *brothers*!" Kate insisted. "Lars is fine, but you're—" She stopped, trying to think of a name she could say in front of Mama and Papa.

Mama held up her hands. "Stop it! Stop it! We'll be grateful if we have a healthy normal baby. That's what you should want too."

Anders pushed his chair away from the table. "Don't want any more dumb girls."

"Anders." Papa spoke sternly. "I don't want to hear you talk about a dumb girl again. And I want you to show respect for your mother."

The tall blond boy closed his mouth. But when Papa stood up to take the Bible from the shelf, Anders tipped back in his chair. Behind his father's back, he smirked at Kate.

Kate turned her head and pretended she didn't see. But she felt last night's rush of anger. As Papa read the chapter for that day, her thoughts leaped far away. It wasn't hard to remember what she'd decided.

I'll show Anders, she promised herself. *Whatever he tries, I'll do better. I'll prove a girl can do anything as well as a boy.*

A moment later Papa closed the Bible, and Kate realized she hadn't heard a word he read.

When Papa finished praying, Mama stayed in her chair instead of starting to work as she usually did. "I wonder," she said quietly, looking at Papa. "I wonder if I've really forgiven my little brother. It still hurts so much when I remember what he did."

As though it were yesterday, Kate thought back to January and the letter Mama had received from Sweden. For days she had walked around, looking sad.

"My little brother Ben," Mama said now. "He did something he never should have done."

Tears welled up in her eyes. Impatiently she brushed them away. "Stealing from a shopkeeper. Running off, no one knows where. Such a black spot on our good family name."

Mama sighed. Placing both hands on the table, she lifted herself from her chair.

As Mama walked over to the cookstove, Kate watched her heavy steps. Until the past few months Kate had never seen her mother look awkward. Any day now the baby would be born.

Thinking about it, Kate felt uneasy. Out here in the country, far away from doctors, it was sometimes hard to get help. If possible, Erik's mother would come. As a midwife, she often helped women have babies. But what if she didn't get here in time?

As Kate washed breakfast dishes, she tried to push aside her uneasiness. Yet one thought kept going around in her mind. *What if something goes wrong?*

4

Surprise for Mama

$\mathcal{A}$s soon as Kate finished the dishes, she went outside to pump fresh water and carry it to the chickens.

When Anders found her near the barn, he pushed back his cap and grinned. "Papa says I'm not supposed to call you a dumb girl. So I won't. I'll just treat you like one."

Kate gasped. "I don't have words to describe you," she sputtered.

Anders laughed. "Well, I can tell you what to say—about yourself, I mean."

Throwing back her shoulders, Kate lifted her chin. *How can I possibly get even?* she wondered. With her head high, she stalked to the house.

At lunchtime she glared at Anders, but refused to speak to him. Every time he spoke, Kate looked down at her plate. When the family finished eating and only she and Mama were left, Kate tried to escape.

Her mother's voice called her back. "Kate!"

Slowly Kate turned.

"Don't go out the door without forgiving the one who hurt you."

"Oh, Mama! Anders is always looking for ways to be mean! I don't *want* to forgive him."

"If you don't, it'll hurt you even more than it does him."

Kate groaned. "How can I possibly forgive him?"

A smile lit Mama's face. "You choose to forgive."

A lump the size of a walnut tightened Kate's throat. "It's all right for you," she said. The words spilled out before she could call them back. "You don't have to live with your brother every day."

"You don't think it costs me anything? To forgive my brother, I mean?" Mama's voice was still quiet, but sparks lit her eyes.

As Kate escaped down the trail to Spirit Lake School, her mother's words seemed to follow her. The more Kate thought about Anders, the more upset she became. "Dumb boy!" she said aloud.

The next moment she caught her breath. She had called Anders the very name he called her! It almost struck her funny.

Almost, but not quite. "That's what he deserves to be called!" Kate's angry voice shouted into the wind. She wasn't going to forgive him. Not until *he* changed.

Choose to forgive? Kate scoffed at the idea. But she couldn't push aside the awful way she felt.

Later that afternoon Kate walked the long trail to the main road and the mailbox. She found just one letter—an envelope addressed to Mrs. Ingrid Lindblom O'Connell Nordstrom. Someone certainly knew all of Mama's names.

The letter was written in a script that looked as though its writer lived in Sweden. But there was no return address. And the postmark read, "Duluth, Minnesota."

Kate hurried home with the letter. She found Mama sitting with Anders and Papa at the kitchen table.

Mama looked at the postmark, then turned the letter over in her hands. "Who can it be?" she asked.

"Well, maybe you should open it," Papa said gently. "I think you'll find out."

Mama laughed. "Yah, Carl, you might be right."

As Papa emptied his coffee into a saucer, Mama poured another cup for herself. Then she slit the envelope open with a knife and pulled out the single sheet of paper.

Mama glanced down at the signature. Her smile disappeared.

"It's Ben," she said, and her voice trembled. "My little brother Bernhard."

Kate bit her lip. She remembered how many times Mama had been upset because of Ben. As far as her mother knew, no one had heard from him since he ran away.

As Mama read the letter, her lips moved, but no sound escaped. When she looked up, tears stood in her eyes. Quickly she brushed them away.

Mama shook her head, as though not believing what she'd seen. "I must read it to you."

As Mama read aloud, she translated into English for Kate.

Dear Sister Ingrid:

You may be surprised to hear from your youngest brother. I admit I am afraid to write to you. However, you may know the worst about me already.

Eight months ago I stole money from a shopkeeper in our hometown. I had the America fever and ran away. I went over the mountains to Norway. There I bought a ticket and took a ship to New York.

While on the ship I suffered a terrible sickness. I nearly died, but I came to myself. I was ashamed of the bad thing I did. When I reached America, I found a job on the docks. I earned the money to repay the shopkeeper and set that right.

I am deeply sorry I disgraced our family name. I have asked God's forgiveness, and now I ask yours. Can you find it in your heart to forgive me?

I am now working in Duluth, Minnesota, and have learned that you live not too far distant. I want to see you, but am afraid you do not want to see me.

People tell me I can cross the St. Croix River at Tennessee Flats near Grantsburg. I will come to the top of the hill on the Minnesota side of the river. I will be there at sundown, 28 March 1907. If you are there to meet me, I will know you want to see me. If you are not there, I will go away and never trouble you again.

> Your youngest brother,
> Bernhard

This time as Mama looked up, she smiled through her tears. "My little brother! Of course, I want to see him!"

Papa's eyes looked thoughtful. "What's the postmark on the letter?"

Mama turned the envelope over. "February 20th."

"That's over a month ago!" exclaimed Papa. "How can a letter take so long to come from Duluth?"

"And today is March 26th!" Suddenly Mama returned to earth. "March 28th is only two days away. We need to get ready!"

Papa shook his head. "A woman who could have a baby at any moment should travel all the way to the St. Croix River?"

"My little brother will be waiting for me," answered Mama. "He'll think I do not care. He'll go away, never to return again."

"Yah, that is true," Papa said, stroking his long brown beard. "But you shall not be there. What if your time comes while you are on the road?"

"I'll go instead of Mama," Kate said quickly. "Anders and I can meet Ben."

Anders grinned. "We'll take Wildfire. If we start early tomorrow, it'll be easy to reach Tennessee Flats by sundown the next day."

"Yah, it might work," said Papa slowly. "Then I can stay with Mama. I'll be here if the baby comes."

"Good! Then it's all settled!" exclaimed Anders. "We'll get ready right away." He started toward the door.

"Just a minute, Anders." Mama's voice called him back. "You can go. But I want you to ask Erik if he can go with you. Kate will stay here."

"Stay *here*?" Kate jumped up so fast that her chair tipped over. She couldn't believe Mama's words.

"Certainly." Mama's voice sounded as though her mind were made up. "I don't want you running around with a timber swindler hiding in the bushes."

"Oh, Mama!" Kate wailed. She looked toward Anders, hoping for his support.

But no responding grin lit his face. Instead, a strange expression darkened his blue eyes.

An awful thought crossed Kate's mind. What if—

From across the room Anders looked at Kate. Their gaze met. Was he wondering the same thing?

Slowly Kate picked up her chair and sat down. As Mama poured Papa another cup of coffee, Kate tried to think things through.

She decided to try again. "Mama, what if something goes wrong?"

"That's what I'm afraid of." Mama's voice sounded brisk.

Kate bit her tongue. She had certainly found a bad way to start. On her next try she was more careful. "Mama, you know I'm good at figuring things out—if there's a mystery or something."

Mama nodded. "Yah." She couldn't deny that.

"If something goes wrong, I can help Anders decide what to do."

Anders made a choking sound.

Kate glared at him. "Maybe I can think of something he wouldn't."

When Mama did not speak, Kate rushed on. "It's really important that we get there in time. If we miss your little brother, even by fifteen minutes, you'll never hear from him again."

"Yah." Again the tears welled up in Mama's eyes. "How awful it would be for him to think that. To think I do not have it in my heart to forgive him."

Kate nodded. "It would wreck Ben's whole life. So I'll help Anders find him."

Anders cleared his throat, but Kate refused to look at him.

Mama sat quietly, thinking about it. "You're right, Kate, two heads are better than one."

Kate sighed with relief.

But Mama wasn't finished. "Anders, you go over and talk to Erik."

Mama turned back to Kate. "If Erik can go, it should be his head and not yours."

"Oh, Mama!" Kate wailed again.

But her mother's mind was made up, and Kate knew it wouldn't do a bit of good to say more. As Anders headed out the door, she pulled on her coat and followed him.

"I want to go with you," Kate said when safely away from the house. "Tell Erik I want to meet Mama's little brother."

Anders pushed back his thatch of blond hair. "Remember, Kate. Mama's little brother is now eighteen years old."

Again Kate felt uneasy. She remembered the strange expression she'd seen on Anders' face. "Are you thinking what I'm thinking?" she asked.

Her brother shrugged. "Well, depends." The look in his eyes told Kate Anders was more concerned than he sounded.

He started for the barn, then stopped and came back. "Are you wondering if Mama's brother has already crossed the river?"

5

Papa's Warning

$\mathcal{K}$ate felt as if a cold March wind had struck her. That's what she was wondering, all right. Even though she and Anders were alone, she spoke softly. "Anders, do you suppose Ben is the timber swindler?"

"I don't know," he said. "Can you remember anything to give us a clue?"

"How the swindler looked, you mean?"

"Yup." For once Anders sounded serious. "It was pretty dark," he said.

"I think he was tall," answered Kate. "And thin. Not heavy around the middle."

"That's what I thought too." Anders squinted into the morning sunlight instead of looking at Kate. "You know what that means."

"I'm afraid so." Kate spoke in a low voice, as if even the nearby bushes could hear. "Some older men stay thin. But some look more—more—heavyset."

"Broad through the shoulders," said Anders. "And thick through the middle."

Kate giggled, but the laughter died on her lips. "The swindler

37

was thin through the waist, wasn't he?"

"But strong in the shoulders," said Anders. "So he could be most any age."

"I think there's something we need to know." Kate spoke slowly. "If we find out that Ben is the swindler, would Mama—" She stopped, hating to even ask the question.

Anders finished for her. "Would Mama want us to bring him home?"

Looking as if he disliked the idea as much as Kate, Anders walked back with her to the kitchen. When he opened the door, Mama and Papa were still at the table. They looked startled, as though they had suddenly stopped talking.

Anders joined them at the table. "Mama, do you have any idea what your brother looks like now?"

Mama glanced at Papa before she answered. "The most recent picture was taken—" Mama stopped to think. "Probably six years ago."

"It's in the trunk?" Kate headed for the dining room.

"On the right side," Mama called after her. "Near the bottom."

Mama had brought this trunk from Sweden at the age of seventeen. On the flat top stood a photograph. Picking it up, Kate studied the faces. She knew the story of the picture well.

Mama's parents sat in the center, surrounded by Mama's five sisters and two brothers. The youngest sister held a framed photograph of Mama.

"So I could still be part of the family," Mama often explained. Soon after coming to America, she'd had the photo taken and sent to her family.

Now Mama's youngest brother interested Kate most—little Bernhard. Two and a half years old at the time his sister arrived in America, he looked blond and chubby and happy.

Kate stared at Ben's round boyish face. How could a boy like that steal from a shopkeeper?

Setting the family photo aside, Kate opened the trunk and searched for the more recent picture of Ben. It was far down, beneath blankets and towels. *Bernhard Lindblom*, it said on the back, along with the date, *1901*.

Ben was still blond, but now he had stretched up. Ben's grin reminded Kate of Anders.

When Kate brought the picture to her mother, Mama gazed at the face without speaking. "Yah, Ben's tall," she said at last. "Like my Papa."

"And thin," said Anders, looking over Mama's shoulder.

"And thin." Mama bit her lip, as though it hurt to look at her brother.

"He's starting to get broad shoulders," Papa said.

"Yah, from the farm work," Mama answered. "Always there was more work than money. The farm was too small for a big family. Papa and Mama worked night and day, but it wasn't enough."

Then Kate noticed something she hadn't seen in the earlier picture. "Ben has a scar on his chin."

Mama looked closer. "You're right, Kate. Something must have happened to him between the two pictures."

As Mama set the picture down, Anders turned to Kate. "You ask," he said.

"No, you." Kate dreaded the idea.

"It's *your* job." Anders sounded unwilling to give in.

"It's *yours*," Kate answered.

Anders shook his head. "She's *your* mother."

Mama looked from one to the other. Her eyes flashed. "And I hope I'm *your* mother, too, Anders. Even though I'm the second one."

Anders flushed, and Mama turned back to Kate. "Now tell me. Just what are you and Anders talking about?"

Kate cleared her throat. "About Ben, Mama." But she couldn't go on.

"Ahhhh!" A light entered Mama's eyes. "Are you wondering if he's the timber swindler?"

Kate felt the warmth of embarrassment creep into her face.

Mama nodded, as if she had her answer. "Carl and I just talked about it." Mama glanced toward Papa, as though needing his support. "We wondered if Ben has already crossed to this side of the St. Croix River."

Mama bit her lip. In her eyes there was something even greater than hurt. Was it worry? Or more? To Kate it seemed as if her mother's heart were being squeezed. Unable to bear the pain in Mama's eyes, Kate looked away.

For long minutes no one spoke. In the stillness Kate heard the tick of the clock in the dining room. Then a piece of wood dropped in the cookstove.

"I want to believe," Mama said at last. She wiped her hand across her eyes.

After a moment she went on. "No, it's more than that. I *do* believe Ben meant what he said in the letter."

Mama drew a deep breath. "When Ben says he's sorry, I have to believe he means it. I have to believe he's changed, unless he shows me he hasn't."

When Mama spoke again, her voice sounded stronger. "Whatever Ben did in Sweden, it's over. It's over because I forgive him."

Grasping the edge of the table, Mama pulled herself up. As she walked from the room, her back was straight, but her shoulders trembled.

———

When Anders returned from talking to Erik, Kate heard the good news. Mr. Lundgren and Erik's older brother were gone, so Erik needed to stay home to do chores.

Mama gave permission for Kate to go with Anders, but a troubled look shadowed her blue eyes. "Anders, there's something you have to promise me," she said.

"Sure, Mama. What is it?" His lopsided grin told Kate that he knew what was coming.

"I want you to promise that you'll take good care of your sister."

Anders lifted his right hand and did his best to put on a straight face. "I solemnly swear, Mama. I'm very good at taking care of Kate."

"I want you to do more than that," Papa added. "I want you to promise that no matter what happens, the two of you stay together."

Anders' smirk disappeared. "Yes, Papa," he said solemnly.

Mr. Nordstrom turned to Kate. "You promise?"

"I promise." Kate looked at Papa because she refused to look at Anders.

When Kate hurried to her room, she felt excited. She had gotten what she wanted, after all. She could go to meet Ben. And there was something more. *I'll prove to Anders I can keep up with anything he needs to do.*

As Kate packed her other dress and a warm sweater, she looked forward to going to Grantsburg. The Nordstrom family traveled the eleven long miles only when there was a real need.

What will it be like? Kate wondered, as she thought about going five miles beyond the village. Kate had been to the St. Croix River only once—when coming to live at Windy Hill Farm.

Now Kate wished that Erik were going along. It was always fun being with him. Yet something else bothered Kate much more.

During the late afternoon, she and Mama worked together, preparing supper. For a time the two of them were alone. Kate cracked butternuts and watched for her chance. Finally she asked, "Mama?"

"Yah?"

Kate looked at a nutshell instead of her mother. "What if the baby comes while I'm gone?"

A smile lit Mama's eyes. "Then I'll have a little one for you when you get back."

"That's not what I mean." Kate tried to choose her words carefully. "What will happen when the baby is born?"

Mama looked surprised. "Why, you know. Papa will go for Erik's mother. She's a good midwife and has promised to help me."

Again Kate hesitated. "I know Mrs. Lundgren is a good midwife, but—" Kate stopped, then went on. "What if—" Once more, words failed her.

Mama sat down next to Kate. "What if something goes wrong? Is that what you're asking?"

Unable to look into Mama's eyes, Kate nodded.

Mama reached out, putting her hand on Kate's arm. When she spoke her voice was gentle. "You're right, Kate, sometimes things go wrong. Out here in the country, I'm far from help. I know that."

"I'm afraid, Mama," Kate whispered.

"Afraid that something will happen to me, yah?"

"Yah." The word sounded strange, coming from Kate. "If something goes wrong, would having a baby be worth it?"

"I believe God wants me to have this new life," Mama said. "I need to trust that He'll take care of me."

Mama took Kate's hand. "Here, Kate. Feel the baby's foot."

At one side there was an extra bulge in Mama's large stomach. As Kate touched that place, she felt a small kick.

Kate laughed, but her mother looked serious. "That's what it's like," Mama said. "That's what it's like to know a little heart beats beneath my ribs."

Mama patted her stomach. "In the whole world there's no other baby who will be exactly like this one. I'm the only person who can give this little one life."

————

That evening Papa sat down at the kitchen table to help Anders and Kate plan their trip.

"You'll have terrible mud for at least part of the way," Papa said. "But you've got two good days to travel. When you get to Grantsburg, go to Walfrid Johnson's and ask if you can stay overnight."

As he finished sharpening a pencil, Papa put down his knife. "If you get up early the next morning, you should have more than enough time to find Ben."

Papa started drawing a map. "There's no bridge over the Wood River between Grantsburg and the St. Croix."

Papa drew a jiggly line showing the Wood River as it flowed through the north side of the village.

"That means you have to cross on the bridge in Grantsburg. Then go north until you turn left here."

Papa drew another line. "If you follow this road, you'll find a bridge across Sand Creek. Someone cut down two big trees and laid them from bank to bank. Small poles cross the trees. They're enough so that Wildfire's hoofs won't go through."

"Won't the creek be frozen?" Kate asked.

"Aw, Kate," said Anders. "Every one knows that if a crick flows fast, it won't freeze in winter." He tipped his head slightly, as though trying to say something without words.

Kate looked beyond Anders to the wood cookstove. Mama stood there, baking cookies for them to take along. She seemed to be listening.

Papa extended a line across the creek. "Keep on this road. Then take a right and a left. You're going west, then north, then west again."

Anders nodded, and Papa began writing. "You'll come to the Berglund farm. Near his house take the trail into the woods, and you'll end up at Tennessee Flats."

"Tennessee Flats?" asked Kate.

"The first settler in that area was a man named Isaac Tennessee."

Kate leaned forward to study the map.

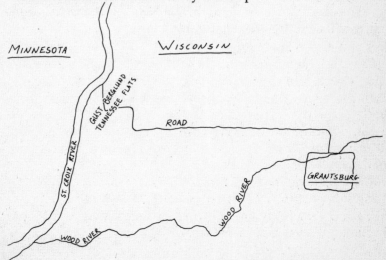

Papa pointed to an area near the St. Croix River. "In the early days people traveled up the Wisconsin side of the river and forded it there."

"What do you mean?" Kate asked. In spite of her desire to make the trip, she was starting to wonder about all that could happen.

"They crossed it," Papa explained. "There's no bridge there, but the river is wide and shallow. In summer there are ferries at other places along the St. Croix. But people used to walk over at Tennessee Flats, or take a team of horses. They stayed on the west side of the river to go to Duluth."

Anders tipped back in his chair, as though sure that he knew the way. "So we cross the river at Tennessee Flats."

As Mama walked into the dining room, Papa lowered his voice. "I hope so."

"What do you mean, you hope so?" asked Kate, her voice just as quiet.

Papa sighed and ran his fingers through his beard. "If the river is still frozen, you'll have no trouble crossing over. If not—"

Anders nodded as his gaze met his father's.

"If not what?" Kate whispered.

"I don't want your mother to worry," said Papa. "She's got enough on her mind right now."

He looked first at Anders, then at Kate. "If the ice has gone out, you'll be in trouble. Big trouble."

6

Growing Evidence

The next morning Kate awoke with a feeling of excitement in her bones. As she went outside, the sun peeked over the horizon.

Already Anders had backed Wildfire between the shafts of the wagon. The mare's black coat and white socks shone in the early light.

The farm wagon looked like an oblong box with the large wooden wheels in back bigger than those in front. Kate climbed up into the wagon bed.

Anders handed her Mama's two baskets of food. Kate knew what they contained—enough of her mother's good brown bread to last for four days, apples from the barrel in the root cellar, carrot sticks, and oatmeal cookies. Mama had made certain they'd eat well.

Carefully Kate covered the food with a heavy horse blanket. She could only hope that if it rained, the blanket would keep the sandwiches and cookies dry.

Anders handed up a wooden box with extra clothes for each of them, as well as more blankets made from the hides of animals. A tool box came next, as well as a hatchet, ax, shovel, and bucket.

"Why do you need all this stuff?" Kate asked.

Anders shrugged. "Well, you never know."

As they finished loading the wagon, Lars started across the yard.

"Bye, Lars," Kate called. Then she jumped down. Her nine-year-old brother had gotten up early just to see them off.

With a coat pulled over his nightshirt, Lars wore boots too big for him. Though the morning sunlight showed the whiteness of his face, Kate felt grateful for his growing strength. She couldn't take that for granted. Not anymore.

"You're a good brother, Lars," she said quietly when Anders went to the other side of the wagon.

Lars flushed. "Yah, sure." He sounded like Anders. Yet his eyes shone, as though Kate's words meant something to him.

Thinking about the pneumonia he'd had, she wanted to say more. With all her heart she wanted to tell him, "I'm glad you're alive. I'm glad you're *you*." But the words stuck in her throat.

Instead she said, "When I get back, we'll read another book together. All right?"

"Sure thing!" Lars answered. His wide grin warmed Kate.

As she turned away, Lars spoke softly, as if he, too, felt afraid Anders would hear. "You're a good sister, Kate."

Her throat tightened. This from the brother who once put a dead mouse in her bed?

"Thanks, Lars," she whispered.

A moment later Tina flung herself at Kate. The little girl rattled a string of words too fast for Kate to catch the Swedish. Yet she understood Tina's hug.

As Tina let go, Kate saw Mama in the kitchen doorway. Her golden blond hair shone in the morning sunlight. Seeing her, Kate felt torn between going and staying.

What if the baby comes while I'm gone? she wondered. *What if Papa needs help, and I'm not here?*

Then Mama hurried forward. Halfway across the yard, she and Kate met. Her mother's arms went around Kate.

"It's important that you go," Mama said softly. "It's important that we're a family for Ben."

For a moment Mama stroked Kate's long black hair. "My job is to have the baby," she said. "It's your job to find my little brother."

Tears welled up in Kate's eyes, and she could not speak. *Strange!* she thought. So often Mama seemed to know what she was thinking.

Her mother followed Kate back to the wagon. Anders' dog lay near the front wheel.

"Are you going to take Lutfisk?" Mama asked. Anders had named the dog after the dried cod that Swedes soak in lye and eat at Christmas.

At the sound of his name, Lutfisk sat up, as though snapping to attention. With brown, black, and white hair, he had tan markings on his face. He tipped his head to one side.

"Well, I don't know," Kate answered. "I'd hate to have him run off and get lost."

"Lutfisk might come in handy," Mama said.

The dog's ears perked up as if he listened in on the conversation.

"Sure, Kate," Anders broke in. "Handy dandy Lutfisk, that's him."

Lutfisk tilted his head the other way. His bright eyes seemed to cling to every word.

"You better take him, Anders," said Mama. "He can protect Kate."

"Protect *me?*" asked Kate.

"From that man who's running around the woods," Mama answered.

Anders pounded his chest. "*I*, her trusty brother, will protect Kate."

Kate glared at him, then remembered. Her mother could still change her mind about letting her go.

"Good idea, Mama." Kate's voice sounded as sweet as she could make it. "We'll take Lutfisk."

"C'mon, boy!" Anders called. "You can go with us!"

Lutfisk leaped to his feet and barked. His tail wagged so fast Kate wondered if it would fall off.

"Did you see that?" Anders asked proudly. "That shows you how much he understands."

As Anders held Wildfire still, the family gathered around the wagon.

"I want to remind you of God's promise," Papa said, looking first at Anders, then at Kate.

Recalling Papa's warning of the night before, Kate stood straighter.

"Joshua needed to cross the Jordan River when it was at flood stage," Papa went on. "God told him, 'Have I not commanded thee? Be strong and of a good courage; be not afraid, neither be thou dismayed: for the Lord thy God is with thee whithersoever thou goest.' "

Again Papa looked long at Kate and Anders, as though wanting to be sure they caught what he was saying. Then he bowed his head.

"We thank thee, Heavenly Father," Papa prayed. "We thank thee that thou wilt be with Kate and Anders when we cannot. We ask thee to give them courage, wisdom, and protection."

For a moment he paused, then said, "Ah-men."

"Ah-men," echoed the others.

Mama cleared her throat, and Papa clapped Anders on the shoulder. "Don't forget your promise to us. Stay together, no matter what happens."

Anders and Kate climbed up and sat down on the high spring seat.

Papa stepped back from the wheels. "Do you have the map?"

Anders patted his shirt pocket and nodded.

Kate started to wave. Instead, a question spilled out. "If the baby comes while we're gone, what are you going to name her?"

Mama looked at Papa. "We're still talking about it. Both of us want to name the baby after someone special."

"Hmmmm," said Anders. "Well, that could be me."

Kate laughed. "I can't believe you said that. Sometimes your—your—" She thought for a moment. "What's the word? Arrogance. Your arrogance amazes me."

Anders winked at Papa, then offered Kate his lopsided grin. "That so?"

"Besides, it's going to be a girl," said Kate. "Can you imagine a girl named Anders?"

Lars snickered. Tina jumped up and down, clapping her hands. Kate wondered if the little girl knew English well enough to understand the joke.

Anders flushed, but refused to give up. "Well, if that awful event occurs, how about something *like* Anders? Andrea, Annabelle, Annie."

This time even Mama laughed. "We'll give it some thought," she said, as though trying to be serious.

Anders turned to Wildfire. "Giddyup!" he called. The high-spirited mare pranced out of the farmyard with Lutfisk running alongside.

Twisting around, Kate waved to Lars and Tina, Papa, and Mama. Then the barn blocked her view.

Tall trees lined both sides of the trail they took to the main road. Here in the woods patches of snow had escaped the sunlight. The iron rim around each wooden wheel left a deep track.

When Kate and Anders reached the main road, they found even deeper ruts cut by passing wagons. Because of below-freezing temperatures the night before, the ground was still firm. Though the wagon bumped up and down, they made good time. Yet Kate knew that as soon as the sun warmed the roads, the dirt would turn to mud.

At first Anders took the way they normally drove to town. Lutfisk ran back of the wagon, now and then disappearing into the bushes. Then Anders turned onto a road Kate hadn't seen before. Before long, the road became a trail.

For some time they traveled without seeing anything but trees. "Where are we?" asked Kate as her uneasiness grew.

"Near the Wood River," Anders told her in a low voice.

A few minutes later he stopped Wildfire, and he and Kate climbed down. "Be quiet," he warned. He snapped a lead rope onto the mare's halter and tied the rope to a tree.

Soon the woods thinned out, and they came to great stacks

of logs. Stopping at the first pile, Anders studied the ends of the logs. He pointed to the sawed edge. "Looks all right to me. They're a bit weathered."

But then he and Kate walked around to the other end, the side away from the trail. Here the ends of the logs were newly sawed and marked.

Anders traced the mark with his finger. "Remember this," he said. "Don't forget even one line."

Turning away, he checked the other piles of wood near the river. In each case, someone had tampered with the logs.

Kate felt uneasy. "There's something I don't understand." She, too, spoke softly, as if someone might hear. "Wouldn't the farmers notice that someone tampered with their logs?"

"Maybe. Maybe not," Anders said. "Look at the ground."

Kate saw what he meant. Whatever sawdust there had been, it was now mixed into the dirt.

"And there's something else. When the men open the dam between Big Wood Lake and Wood River, they want to catch the rush of water. They don't lift the logs into the river one by one. It'd be too much work."

Anders led Kate to the river side of a pile of logs. "See how the logs are set on skids?"

The skids were timbers that slanted down toward the river. Anders pointed to a key piece of wood at the front of the logs.

"When it's time to send the logs downstream, a man stands at each end of the pile. They knock out that piece with a sledge-hammer. They've got to be mighty good jumpers."

"What do you mean?" asked Kate.

"It's dangerous work. The logs tumble into the river. But if one of them goes crossways or gets out of line—"

"It hits the man?" Kate asked.

"It could. Whoever sends the logs into the water gets paid extra. But some of them never collect."

As Kate's uneasiness grew, she glanced around. For some reason the woods seemed darker. Then she looked up between the branches. Murky clouds covered the sun.

"Where do you think the timber swindler is now?" Kate whispered.

"I don't know. Could be most anywhere, I guess." He grinned. "Even looking at us from behind a bush."

Kate didn't think her brother's teasing was funny. "Let's go," she said.

She and Anders hurried back to the wagon. When they climbed up to the high spring seat, Wildfire seemed eager to leave the trees behind.

As they reached the main road, the rain began. Kate doubled the blankets covering the food.

"This will take care of any leftover snow," Anders said.

At first a cold drizzle filled the deep ruts in the road. Then the dampness seeped through the heavy blanket Kate pulled over her coat.

Soon Lutfisk leaped into the back of the wagon and crept forward to where Kate and Anders sat. As the rain increased, the ruts in the road softened and the mud grew deeper. The wagon wheels lurched down, in and out of potholes.

The cold rain entered Kate's bones. "How much farther?" she asked finally.

"Three or four miles," Anders told her.

A moment later the rain moved like a wall of water against them. Kate pulled a blanket over her head until only her eyes showed.

As the rain pelted them, Wildfire plodded on. Muddy water splattered up around the wagon. Kate's teeth chattered.

Anders looked down at her. "Your teeth rattling in your head, Kate?"

In spite of her misery, Kate giggled. It seemed only a moment since that muddy March day a year before. On that terrible trip, she and Mama had come from Minneapolis. In mud like this, Anders had asked the same question.

After a long stretch of potholes, the rain eased, then stopped. Kate pulled out sandwiches. Soon they finished the apples and carrots. But it was all right, Kate told herself. Plenty of cookies and bread remained.

Before long, they came to a partly cleared field dotted with large stumps. The ground was less chewed up, and Anders directed Wildfire off the road. As he guided the mare between the stumps, the wagon jolted up and down. Even so, they made better time.

Then the field ended. Trees and underbrush blocked the way. Anders directed Wildfire back to the road.

Once again they lurched through deep ruts. As a front wheel dropped into a hole, Wildfire strained forward, then stopped.

"Giddyup!" Anders called. "C'mon, girl! Move out."

Wildfire's beautiful black coat was brown with mud. As far ahead as Kate could see, the road looked bottomless.

"Giddyup!" Anders urged the horse again.

This time the wagon moved, and Kate was glad she was riding instead of walking.

Yet as they came out of the hole, she glanced down.

"Oh, Anders!" she exclaimed. "Look at the wheel!"

7

The Stranger

*A*s Kate stared, the iron rim circling the outer edge of the wheel wobbled. From side to side it moved. Then the rim separated from the wood underneath.

Quickly Anders turned Wildfire to the side of the road. But trees grew close to the trail, offering no place to go.

The rim slipped crossways at a right angle to the wheel. "It's coming off!" Kate warned.

Anders tugged the reins and managed to stop the wagon before the rim fell to the ground.

Kate sighed with relief. But she knew their trouble was only beginning.

Anders moaned. "Always thought rims came off wheels in dry weather. 'Course these awful roads don't help."

He ran his fingers through his thatch of blond hair. "Come to think of it, an old-timer told me it can happen any time of year. Especially in spring, when a wagon hasn't been used all winter."

"So what do we do?" asked Kate.

"Get the wheel to a blacksmith."

"A blacksmith?" Kate stared at the mud surrounding the

wagon. If she climbed down, that oozing brown water would go over the top of her boots.

"A blacksmith," Anders said again.

"Can you tell me how we get to a blacksmith?"

"Nope," said Anders. "The closest one is at least three miles away. But if I use the wheel without the rim, I'll wreck it. And that's big money."

He stared down at the mud, then at the long stretch of road. From the look on his face, Anders didn't like the idea of walking any better than Kate. In either direction there was no one in sight.

"I've got a pliers," Anders said after some thought. "And some other tools, but—" Again he looked at the mud around them.

"There's only one thing to do," he said finally. Crawling behind the seat, Anders found the pliers, then slipped over the side of the wagon.

With his first step he sank deep in mud. With his next step the mud oozed over the top of his boots. With every step after that, the mud sucked at his boots and splattered his clothes.

"You better stay there," he called as he reached firmer ground. Boots and pants brown with mud, he stood at the edge of the road.

"Stay here!" exclaimed Kate. "What choice do I have?"

Then she caught her brother's grin. At least he was the one getting dirty.

As Anders stretched out his long legs, Lutfisk stood up in the back of the wagon. With one look at Anders, the dog jumped off the end. When he landed, the mud sprayed up, covering him.

Kate groaned, but Anders laughed. "C'mon, boy!" he called, and the dog went to him.

Anders stayed along the trees, and Lutfisk followed close on his heels. Before many minutes passed, they became two small dots, far ahead. Then they disappeared.

As time grew long, Kate looked at the woods. The trees seemed to move closer by the minute. In spite of the mud, she wished she had gone with Anders.

Then a breeze stirred the bushes.

"I refuse to be afraid," Kate said aloud. Yet she couldn't help but think about the timber swindler. What if he were nearby? What if he suddenly appeared? There was no place to go. Except through mud, that is.

Then against the horizon a small dot appeared, then another. Was that Anders and Lutfisk?

As Kate watched, the dots grew larger. Soon she could see her brother and the dog.

When Anders reached the wagon, he held up a long piece of wire.

"Where'd you get it?" Kate asked as he pushed the rim back over the wood.

"Found a barbed-wire fence," said Anders. Wrapping the wire around the rim, he passed it between the spokes of the wheel.

"You cut a barbed-wire fence?" asked Kate. "The cattle will get out!"

"Nope. Barbed wire has a double strand. I cut the wire without barbs and unwound it. I'll buy new wire in town and fix the fence when we come back."

Carefully Anders wound the wire until it held the rim against the wooden circle of the wheel. At last he threw the pliers into the tool box and climbed up to the seat.

Mud covered his overalls well past his knees. As he sat down, Kate moved as far away as possible.

Lutfisk barked, wanting to get up. But the dog was so dirty Kate wouldn't let him near the wagon.

When they reached Grantsburg's main street, Anders turned right toward Walfrid Johnson's. The family lived on the second floor of a large frame building. Beneath, on the ground floor, was Mr. Johnson's blacksmith shop. Anders stopped Wildfire close to the large open door.

As Kate climbed down from the wagon, she felt glad to be on solid ground again. When Mr. Johnson came outside, Anders explained what had happened.

Taking a jack, the blacksmith raised the heavy wagon and

slipped off the wheel. When he rolled it into the shop, Kate saw a tall thin boy standing along the wall.

"Stretch!" she exclaimed.

The boy turned and grinned. But somehow he seemed to have changed.

"How're you doing?" Kate asked.

More than a month before, Stretch had been badly hurt at the Trade Lake Creamery. When he was unloading ice, a large chunk crashed down the ramp, smashing his hand against another block of ice.

"Just came in on the train from Minneapolis," he said.

"You saw a doctor there?" Anders asked.

Stretch nodded. "For the second time. Mr. Swenson took me right after the accident." Since Christmas Stretch had lived at Swenson's farm with Josie's parents and her eight brothers and sisters.

Kate remembered her fright on the day of the accident. The buttermaker had rushed Stretch to the doctor. He had sent Stretch to another doctor in Minneapolis.

Now Kate noticed that the tall thin boy held his injured hand behind his back. "Are you having trouble?" she asked. "Is that why you went back to Minneapolis?"

Again Stretch nodded. He seemed quieter, without his usual swagger.

"What did the doctor say?" Anders asked.

Stretch shrugged. "To give it time."

Kate still wondered what was wrong. Although Stretch and Anders didn't always get along, Stretch usually liked talking with her. Usually he had plenty to say.

Today Kate felt like a dentist with a tooth—pulling information out of him. "Are your fingers all right?" she asked.

"Well, sorta," Stretch answered. "The breaks are healing." Just the same, he kept his hand behind his back.

"What are you afraid to tell us?" Kate asked.

A shadow flickered across Stretch's face. He pulled back.

Anders stepped forward. "Hey, we're friends, Stretch, remember?"

Kate was surprised. Not long ago there'd been bad feelings between the two boys.

For a moment Stretch met Anders' gaze. Stretch was the first to look away.

"Friends?" he asked. His laugh sounded hard and brittle. "What good will that do?"

"What do you mean?" asked Kate. Then she remembered Stretch's dream. Was that why he stood in this shop, watching Walfrid Johnson work?

The tall boy's eyes looked dark with pain. "I ain't sure if I can ever be a blacksmith. I ain't sure if I can ever have my own shop."

Slowly, as though it were the last thing he wanted to do, Stretch withdrew his hand from behind his back. He held it out for Kate and Anders to see.

Kate winced. Stretch's thumb and one of his fingers looked almost normal. But the other three fingers curled back toward the palm of his hand.

"Doc says I hurt the tendons," Stretch said without looking at Anders or Kate.

Swallowing hard, Kate stole a glance at her own hands. She thought about how she liked to play the organ. And how much she needed her hands to play.

"Is it permanent?" asked Anders when Kate could not speak. "Maybe it needs more time, like Doc says."

"Don't know yet," said Stretch. "I can't do nuthin' with it." Again he put his hand behind his back.

Again Kate swallowed, trying to push aside the lump in her throat. She wished she knew what to say. All she could think of was "I'm sorry." But Stretch seemed to understand.

When Anders finished talking to Walfrid Johnson, he went around to the pump. There he washed off Wildfire and Lutfisk and the worst of the mud on himself. Then he and Kate climbed the outside stairs.

Halfway up, Kate stopped. "Did Papa give you money?" she asked.

"Yup," said Anders. "But not enough for fixing a wheel and

getting barbed wire, and paying to stay overnight. I'll do the talking."

"Oh, you will?" asked Kate, wondering how he'd handle this.

At the top of the stairs a short woman answered the door. When she heard what Anders wanted, she said, "Come in, come in. We'd like to have you stay with us."

Then she explained. "During the school year, we rent one room to girls from the country. They go to high school in Grantsburg. Kate, you can sleep in their room."

Mrs. Johnson opened the door wider. "We use the other bedroom for our family," she went on. "But Anders, you're welcome to the floor in the dining room."

Anders nodded and looked glad to use the floor. "But your husband is fixing our wagon, and we're almost out of money. Can Kate help you in the kitchen—with the meal and washing dishes?"

Kate stared at him. No wonder Anders wanted to do the talking.

"Certainly, certainly," said Mrs. Johnson.

Anders grinned. "Good. I'll take care of some things in town and be back in time for supper."

When Anders started down the stairs, Kate hurried after him. "Me too," she called to Mrs. Johnson. "I'll be back in time to help."

As soon as Mrs. Johnson could no longer hear, Kate exploded. "Anders, you are the meanest big brother I've ever had!"

"The *only* big brother, you mean," Anders said calmly.

"I wanted to look around town."

"That's what we're doing right now." Anders led her to the fire hall, where they found Big Gust.

The village marshall listened carefully to their story of the damaged logs they'd spotted earlier in the day. Big Gust then said, "I want you to tell Charlie Saunders." The county sheriff owned a harness shop and livery stable near the railroad tracks.

As they walked down the hill with the tall marshall, Anders

turned to Kate. "Once the sheriff ordered four hundred wild horses from out West."

Big Gust's deep laugh rumbled. "When the village board heard about it, they quickly passed an ordinance. Made it against the law to break horses on village streets."

"Kate, you should see Charlie's wife," Anders went on. "She shoots like Annie Oakley. Now that's something you haven't tried."

"Maybe *she'll* be sheriff someday," said Kate.

When Anders laughed, Kate insisted. "She'd be the first woman sheriff in all of Wisconsin!"

When they entered the harness shop and stable, Kate looked around. In addition to selling horses, Mr. Saunders rented them out. He also sold blankets, robes, whips, curry combs, and brushes.

As Anders told the sheriff about the logs along the river, Charlie stroked his handlebar mustache.

"Will you draw the end mark for me?" he asked.

Using the paper he gave her, Kate put down the design she had seen.

Anders agreed that she had it right. "We thought the mark could stand for Wood River or wild river."

"Hmmmm," said Charlie. "The swindler's using a different log mark this time. I wonder how many marks he has registered? Any idea who the man could be?"

For an instant Kate hesitated. Unwilling to speak of their

concern about Ben, she glanced at Anders. He seemed to feel the same way.

"He's tall," said Kate after a moment. "Strong shoulders, thin through the middle. It was dark when we saw him, but his hat looked black."

"Could be a lot of people," said the sheriff. "But I'll see what I can do."

When they left the livery stable, Anders led Kate toward the Antler's Hotel. "Something there I want you to see," he said.

The minute Kate entered the lobby, she knew what her brother meant. Along one wall stood a tall upright piano. Kate forgot all the mud and cold of the day. She even forgot how upset she'd been with Anders.

"Can I play it?" she asked him.

"Ask him." Anders tipped his head toward a man behind the counter.

When he gave permission, Kate sat down on the three-legged stool. Finding it far too low, she stood up and twirled it higher, then settled herself again.

The ivory keys were new and white against the black. It would be different than playing her reed organ, Kate knew. Yet with all her heart she wanted to try. Reaching out an uncertain hand, she sounded one note.

Anders laughed. "You can do better than that."

Kate felt a hot flush creep into her face. She wished that just once her brother would leave her alone.

What can I play? she wondered. With no music it had to be something she knew from memory. Or something she could play by ear.

Then Kate knew. A Swedish folk song, "Children of the Heavenly Father." With all that had gone wrong that day, she needed the promise of God's care.

Placing her hands above the keyboard, Kate started to play. At first the notes sounded choppy and uneven. Then Kate found the pedal and figured out how to use it. Before long, the melody sang.

She couldn't count the times she'd played the song before,

yet now it meant something new. She and Anders were far from home, off on their own. Here, where Mama and Papa couldn't help them, there was someone who could—their heavenly Father.

Kate played the song through, then started over. After several more times, she felt good inside, even peaceful.

When at last she stood up, Kate thought Anders had disappeared. Instead, he waited near the door.

As the two of them left the hotel, she glanced down the street. Ahead of them, a man with a clean-shaven face leaned against a building.

Anders started toward him, and the man straightened up. From his tall height he looked down. His icy blue gaze met Kate's.

Without thinking, she stopped in the middle of the board walk. Anders kept going.

Kate blinked, but the man did not. Beneath a black hat and bushy eyebrows, his stare seemed fixed in place.

8

Sand Creek

*K*ate looked away, then back. Deep furrows lined the stranger's face. His cold eyes seemed dark, even evil.

Kate tried to hurry past him, but her feet felt weighed down, leaden.

Halfway down the block, she glanced around. Even at this distance, the man watched her. A chill slid down Kate's spine.

Anders called to her. "C'mon, Kate! What's keeping you?"

Feeling as if she'd wakened from a nightmare, Kate flipped her long braid over her shoulder. It seemed forever before she caught up to her brother.

"Let's get going," she whispered. Forcing herself not to run, she walked as quickly as possible.

"What's the matter?" Anders asked when they were a full block away. "You're white as a ghost!"

Kate tried to laugh, but the sound died on her lips. "I feel like I've seen a ghost. Did you notice the man back there?"

"The one against the wall?"

Kate nodded. "I know him. I don't know where. But he knows me."

She trembled. "Did you see him stare? When I looked at him, he wouldn't look away. He just kept staring."

A strand of hair blew into Kate's eyes. When she reached up to push it aside, her hand shook.

But Anders grinned. "Oh, Kate, you're just making things up."

"Making things up? How can you say such a thing? You saw the man. Didn't you see the way he stared at me?"

"Nah. He's just watching two good-looking Swedish kids walk down the street."

Kate tried to ignore her scared feelings. "One good-looking Swedish boy and a beautiful Swedish-*Irish* girl," she said. "Don't forget the Irish part of me!"

But her attempt to shrug aside her fear didn't work. Her memory of the stranger's cold eyes was too frightening.

"Anders, I can't remember where I've seen that man. But somehow I know him. He scares me."

"Aw, Kate! I've told you before. You've got too much imagination."

"No, I don't!" Kate was certain about her feelings. "Whoever that man is, he's trouble."

In spite of her best effort to stop, she still trembled. She wished she could forget the icy look in the man's eyes.

Together Kate and Anders continued down the street. When they reached the blacksmith shop, they found Big Gust talking to Walfrid Johnson. Often the marshall ate meals with the Johnson family.

"*God dag!*" the gentle giant greeted them. "So we see you again. And you had a problem with a wheel. Well, it's about ready now."

As Kate and Anders watched, the blacksmith rolled the wheel outside. When he tried to place it on the wagon, the axle slid off the jack.

Mr. Johnson jumped back out of harm's way. But the axle lay on the ground.

The blacksmith took up the jack. Before he could put it in place, Big Gust stepped forward. Bending down, he picked up the heavy wagon as if it were a match stick. Holding it steady, he waited until Mr. Johnson slipped the wheel into position.

When they left the shop, Anders and Kate followed Big Gust and the blacksmith up the outside stairs and into the dining room.

"I hope we aren't too many for you," Kate said politely when they all gathered around the table.

"Nonsense! Nonsense!" Mrs. Johnson threw up her hands. "Where there's room in the heart, there's room in the home."

After Kate did the dishes, she and Anders took another walk down Grantsburg's main street. This time Big Gust was lighting the carbide streetlamps.

"We should tell him about that man this afternoon," said Kate.

But Anders laughed at her. "You can't report someone just because he looks at you the wrong way."

Leaving the main street behind, they walked up the hill to the large red-brick jail. Nearby stood the county courthouse, and next to that, the small wooden jail that was no longer used.

When they walked back downtown again, Big Gust was gone. Kate looked around, wondering if she'd spot the staring stranger. One part of her wanted to see him again. Another part felt afraid that she would.

When she and Anders returned to the Johnson home, the sun had slipped below the horizon. Electricity had come on. In the dining room one bulb hung down at the end of a wire.

"We have over 600 lights in the village now," Mrs. Johnson told them proudly.

The electricity would stay on until midnight. Then the lights would blink as a signal that they were about to go off.

Kate looked at the bright bulb hanging from the ceiling. A long string dangled from the socket that held the bulb. When Kate pulled the string, the light went off. When she pulled it again, the light went on.

"Can you imagine what it would be like, having electricity all the time?" Kate asked. On the farm she'd grown used to facing the sun to see what she was doing. At night she turned toward a kerosene lamp.

For once Anders didn't laugh. His eyes looked thoughtful. "Maybe someday we'll use electricity for everything. If the lines come our way, I'll figure out how to string a wire. We could have lights in the barn."

Kate giggled. "Do you think the cows would like it?"

But Anders was serious. "Can you imagine what it would be like having a machine for milking cows?

Kate shook her head. "No, I can't." It was hard enough for her to milk cows by hand. Even with all her imagination, she couldn't think how to use electricity.

But Anders could. "Maybe I ought to be an inventor," he said. "I'd think up newfangled things."

"To help you get out of work," Kate teased.

Anders grinned. "Yah, sure, to get out of work." But as he pulled the light off, then on, he had a faraway look.

To Kate it seemed he was seeing down through the years. More than once he'd figured out a way to do things—things she couldn't dream of doing.

Her brother's grin disappeared. "If I become an inventor, I won't leave the farm. I want to stay, no matter what. I want to live there all my life."

————

The sky was overcast when Kate came out of the Johnson house the next morning. Standing at the top of the stairs, she studied the clouds. What if it rained again? She wanted to see new places, but didn't look forward to another cold day.

When Kate reached the bottom of the steps, Anders set the baskets of food inside the wagon. Next came a wooden box with their extra clothes. Kate covered everything with heavy horse blankets, then sat down on the high spring seat.

Anders finished harnessing Wildfire and climbed up beside her. He flicked the reins, and whistled for Lutfisk. The dog raced around the corner of the house.

Stepping high, the black mare pranced down the dirt street. Near the Antler's Hotel, Anders turned north past the mill pond. Soon Wildfire crossed the bridge over the Wood River. Farther on, Anders directed her west toward Tennessee Flats.

Before long, the sun broke through the clouds, warming Kate's back. "At least we won't have to sit in wet clothes all day," she said as they came over a rise in the road.

"Don't talk too soon," her brother warned. A worried frown creased his forehead.

Then Kate saw what he meant. At the bottom of the hill, water covered the road.

Anders shook his head, as though unable to believe what he saw.

"This is Sand Creek?" Kate asked. Both upstream and down, trees and bushes stood in water. The dirt road disappeared into what looked like a large lake.

Pulling up Wildfire, Anders studied the situation. "Must be all that rain we had yesterday. Plus the snow melting real fast. I bet it's never been this high before!"

Kate's stomach tightened. The swiftly moving water hid whatever tree trunks and poles served as a bridge. Or had they been washed out? It was impossible to tell.

Some distance beyond the swollen creek, the road reappeared, partway up the hill.

Finally Anders pointed. "That must be the center of the crick. The water moves fastest there. If we drive straight out—"

He dropped his hand, lining up the closest part of the road with the road that emerged on the far side. "If we drive straight through, we should find the bridge."

"*If?*" Kate asked. "It's a long way across. And that water looks deep!"

"It is," he answered. "If I miss the bridge, we're in trouble. Like Papa says, big trouble."

Kate stared at the swirling water, as though it were an enemy. Then she realized it really was an enemy—one that could keep them from reaching Ben on time.

After another long look at the water, Anders clucked to Wildfire. As the mare stepped out, Anders guided her in a straight line toward the road on the far side.

Soon Wildfire's feet splashed in shallow water. Before long, the creek rose to her knees. The mare paused and looked around.

Anders flicked the reins, and Wildfire kept on. She walked carefully, feeling her way. The water surrounded the wheel hubs, reaching upward to the wagon bed.

Suddenly Wildfire froze, as though unwilling to take another step.

"Anders!" Kate warned.

"I know," he said. "But we can't go back."

He clucked to the mare. "Go on, girl!"

Wildfire turned her ears to the sound of his voice. But as she struggled forward, she stumbled.

"Must have stepped in a washout," Anders muttered, his voice tense. "Keep moving, girl!" He slapped the reins. "C'mon!"

The water lapped at the mare's belly. As though testing her footing, she stretched out one leg, then another.

In the next moment, Wildfire found better ground, but Anders pulled off his coat.

Kate looked down. In spite of the high wheels, water pushed against the boards of the wagon bed. A strong current swirled around them.

"Go on, Wildfire," Anders called. "Go on, girl!"

He handed the reins to Kate. "If the water gets any deeper, she can't swim. Not with the wagon. Not against this current."

"The wagon will pull her down?" Kate couldn't imagine anything worse than watching the mare drown.

Anders pulled off his boots and dropped them on the seat. Then he took the reins again.

The water of the main channel swept strong and cold against the mare's chest. In the next instant she wavered.

Kate clutched the seat. "Has the bridge washed out? Or did we miss it?"

Anders didn't answer. Whatever they had done, Wildfire had lost her footing. Thrashing in the water, she fought the stream. Instead of moving forward, she slipped sideways.

In the next instant Anders threw the reins at Kate and jumped off the wagon. As water sprayed up, he vanished into the creek.

Kate waited, her gaze on the spot where her brother went

down. The water was deep here. Too deep. Had Anders hit his head, jumping in?

Fighting against fear, Kate started to pray.

Then Anders surfaced. Treading water, he tossed his head to get the hair out of his eyes. But the current washed against him, carrying him downstream.

Once again Anders disappeared.

9

Lonely Meeting

$\mathcal{K}$ate's hands clenched the reins. Her brother was a good swimmer. But could he handle the strong current, weighed down by clothes? Could he survive the ice-cold water?

As Kate stared at the place where Anders went down, panic overwhelmed her. Where was he?

Again Kate prayed. "Help him, Jesus. Help him!"

A moment later, her brother's blond head appeared above the water. As though he'd received extra strength, Anders fought the current, trying to reach his horse.

A short distance away, the mare thrashed in the water. Her eyes rolled in terror. As the wagon slipped sideways, it pulled Wildfire down.

Kate had all she could do to hold on. Then she saw Anders swimming toward the horse.

He reached for her bridle, but the mare's legs thrashed. Anders was forced to back off.

A moment later Wildfire found solid footing. Anders grabbed her bridle. Leaning into the harness, the mare surged ahead. Her large body rose from the swollen creek.

Leading Wildfire, Anders staggered up the sloping bank. Water streamed out the back of the wagon.

"We made it!" cried Kate. But her brother barely turned his head. He looked too tired to stand.

Hanging on to the bridle, Anders stumbled along the side of the creek. When he reached the dirt road, he started up the slope, then stopped the mare.

Wrapping his arms around Wildfire's neck, he hugged her. "Good girl!" Then Anders collapsed on the ground.

Suddenly Kate remembered Lutfisk. As she jumped down from the wagon, she saw the dog swimming across the creek. When he came up out of the water, he shook his body and sprayed Kate. Finding Anders, he licked his master's face.

Here the soil was sandy, the patch of earth dry. Anders lay there, too exhausted to move. His face looked gray white, his lips blue with cold.

Kate gave him his coat, and he sat up long enough to peel off his wet shirt. In the brisk morning air, he trembled, unable to stop his shivering. His hair dripped water.

Kate pulled off her own coat. "Rub your head," she said, then hurried to the wagon.

There she found every blanket wet. Quickly she searched the wooden box. When she discovered dry clothes for Anders, she felt she'd received a miracle.

As Kate gave him the clothes, he said, "We've got to rub down Wildfire."

"First you need a fire," Kate answered. "Where are the matches?"

"In the tool box." Anders spoke through chattering teeth.

Kate found the matches dry and safe inside a watertight tin. She had never built a fire outside, only within stoves. Now there was no choice.

Trees lined both sides of the road. As Kate headed into them, she moved quickly, searching for kindling.

The undergrowth was still wet from yesterday's rain. In protected places Kate managed to find the small sticks and dry leaves she needed. She carried them to Anders and found he'd pulled on dry clothes.

Kate hurried back to the woods for larger branches. When she returned a second time, Anders sat with knees pulled up, his arms trembling.

"Anders! Stand up!" Kate said. "Stamp your feet! Get moving!"

When he obeyed, Kate guessed how terrible he felt. Her six-foot brother bossed her around so often that it seemed strange telling him what to do. Even stranger to have him obey.

When Anders sat down again, he pulled Kate's coat over his wet head, but continued to shake.

On a patch of dirt a safe distance from the trees, Kate mounded the kindling she'd found. Lighting a match, she held it against the leaves and twigs. The small flame flickered, then went out.

Again Kate lit a match. Again the wind caught the flame before it took hold.

A third time Kate tried. A third time the wind blew out the match.

With each unsuccessful attempt Kate's panic increased. At last she sat back and stared at the small metal box. Only three matches left. She couldn't afford to lose even one more.

She looked at Anders sitting with a coat over his head. "Help me!" she wanted to cry out. But a nagging thought bothered her. Like a small voice it came. *Remember? You were going to keep up to Anders. You were going to do anything he could do.* Now Kate wasn't so sure.

Just then Anders pulled the coat off his head. "Turn your back to the wind," he said.

Kate moved to the other side of her small mound. Kneeling down to shelter the flame from the wind, she struck a match. This time the flame held. The leaves caught fire.

Carefully Kate added small branches, then larger ones. As they, too, caught fire, she sat back, filled with relief.

Anders crawled next to the fire, lay down, and huddled close. Even as Kate watched, he seemed to grow warmer.

When the fire burned steadily, she took long grass and rubbed down Wildfire. Like Anders, Kate couldn't help but hug the horse. Then she went to the carefully packed baskets of food.

As she opened the sandwiches, the bread fell apart. When she tried to pick up a cookie, it broke into mush.

Kate felt sick. "Our food!" she wailed. "It's soaking wet!"

"Forget the food!" Anders growled.

"But what are we going to do?" asked Kate. "We lost all our cookies and sandwiches for the next two days!"

"Forget it!" said Anders again. "We made it with our lives."

As the fire reached upward, Kate spread the wet clothes around it, then went searching for more branches.

This time she needed to go deeper into the trees. Oak grew here and jack pine freshly green with spring. Yet Kate found it difficult to find dry branches.

The farther she walked, the more uneasy she felt. *Bears,* she thought. *There are bears in these woods.* Only two nights ago Anders had wondered if bears had spooked the horses.

Now as Kate searched for wood, a squirrel chattered as though scolding her. A tree grew in a strange shape, and Kate stopped in her tracks. Then, directly in front of her, a bird flew up. Kate jumped, and her heart pounded.

It's only a partridge, she told herself. But it took a long time before her heart stopped thumping.

With each delay in not finding wood, Kate felt more uneasy. If she didn't get back soon, the fire would go out. But she couldn't find windfalls—branches on the ground—of a size she could carry.

She was almost ready to give up when she noticed a jack pine with its sharply pointed needles. On the lower part of the tree, the bare sticks left by dead branches stuck out from the trunk.

Even with Kate's short height, the dead branches were within reach. Best of all, they were dry.

Breaking off one stick, then another, Kate gathered an armload. Turning away from the tree, she started back to Anders.

Just then the nearby bushes seemed to sway in the wind.

But there's no wind here, thought Kate. She was too far into the woods.

She stared at the bushes. Still leafless from winter, the thick, brown branches reached up, almost as high as her head.

Was that a movement? Kate thought so. In that moment she remembered Papa. *He told us to stay together.*

It was too late now. Here she was, all alone.

Again the bushes swayed, this time so suddenly that Kate had no doubt about it. *There's something there, all right.*

In the next instant a large shape moved closer to the branches.

Kate gasped.

Whatever it was, it moved again. Through the lighter brown of the bushes, it looked black.

Kate dropped the sticks she'd gathered. Step by step, she edged away, walking backward. Maybe if she was quiet enough, the bear would not see her. Maybe she could escape.

The next instant Kate backed into a tree, slamming into the bark.

"Owww!" she cried out in surprise. And then, "Anders!"

But her brother was too far away. He could not possibly hear.

10

More Trouble

$\mathcal{K}$ate clapped a hand over her mouth. Something large was coming this way, moving fast. Had it heard her cry for help?

Moving around the tree, Kate started to run. As she turned to look back, the animal walked out of the bushes.

Kate stared. On its large black side, the animal had a few white blotches. Slowly it raised its head and mooed.

A cow!

Kate started to laugh. On farms without barbed-wire fences, cattle often wandered into the woods. Often it was difficult for owners to find them.

"C'mon, bossy," Kate said. Walking forward slowly, she kept talking.

The cow mooed again. Kate petted her neck, then walked away. The cow seemed eager to follow.

After picking up the wood she had dropped, Kate started back to Anders. As if she and Kate were longtime friends, the cow plodded behind, her bell jangling.

As they came out of the woods, Anders sat cross-legged, with hands stretched out to the fire. When he asked, "Are you Mary with her little lamb?" he seemed like his old self.

Kate grinned. "There's no fleece as white as snow." It felt good to see her brother back to normal.

"Hasn't been milked for a while," he said. "She looks mighty uncomfortable. Think we better help her out."

Using the bucket from the wagon, he knelt down next to the cow and started milking. He offered Kate the warm frothy milk, and she drank deeply. She couldn't remember when something tasted so good.

Anders milked some for himself, then set the bucket in a shallow part of the stream. The cold water lapped against the sides of the pail, cooling the milk.

For a time Anders warmed himself by the fire. When Lutfisk grew tired of sitting next to him, he found a stick and brought it to Kate.

"He wants to play," Anders said. "Give it a toss, and he'll fetch it."

Kate threw the stick as far as she could.

Lutfisk raced off. A minute later he was back to drop the stick at her feet. Several times more he brought it to Kate.

"Want to see something else?" Anders asked. "Take the shovel and leave it somewhere. I'm training Lutfisk to bring me tools."

Kate took the shovel from the wagon and showed it to the dog. While Anders held him, Kate hid the shovel in the dry, brown grass on the other side of the road.

"Go get it!" Anders commanded.

Like a streak of lightning, the dog tore across the road. Finding the shovel, he picked up the handle in his teeth. As he started toward Anders, the end of the handle dragged in the dirt.

Lutfisk dropped the shovel. He nosed along the handle, then picked it up. This time both ends of the shovel stayed off the ground.

"Did you see that?" Anders asked proudly. "He's figured out how to balance the weight in his mouth!"

"Pretty smart dog," Kate admitted.

As the fire died down, Kate tied a rope around the cow's neck and fastened the rope to the back of the wagon.

Anders brought buckets of water from the creek. After drowning the top layer of ashes, he pushed them aside with the shovel. He soaked the hot coals underneath, then held his hand about two inches above the wet pile.

"I still feel heat!" he exclaimed.

Taking several more trips, Anders poured on water until the coals and ashes felt cold to his touch.

When Kate and Anders returned to the wagon, they helped Lutfisk up to the high spring seat. Sitting between them, the dog faced the road, almost seeming human.

Anders clucked to Wildfire. "Tennessee Flats, here we come!" The wagon rolled ahead, and the cow plodded behind.

Anders looked at the sun. Already it was well on its way toward the middle of the sky. "Lost too much time," he grumbled. "If everything goes all right, we'll be in good shape. If not—"

As they continued up the slope in the road beyond Sand Creek, Kate glanced back. Just looking at the swirling water scared her. What if she'd had to break bad news to Papa? What if she'd had to tell him, "Anders drowned in the creek"?

Kate tried not to think about it. Yet Anders also turned for a last glimpse. Kate saw the expression on his face.

Then, as she glanced beyond the swollen water, her eye caught a sudden movement. What was it?

Kate stared in that direction. Whatever it was seemed to fade into a tree. Was someone following them? She couldn't be sure.

Soon the road evened out into two deep ruts stretching far ahead. Kate sneaked another look at her brother. His thatch of blond hair went this way and that, and a streak of mud crossed his nose. But right now he seemed more special than usual.

I'll be nicer to him, Kate told herself, not realizing how hard that promise would be to keep.

At the first farmhouse they spotted they left the cow with the grateful owners.

"Do you think the river will still be frozen?" Kate asked as they continued on their way.

"Maybe." Anders shrugged, as though not wanting to borrow trouble. "Depends."

"What do you mean, *depends*? If the creek is running, will the river be running too?"

"Nope, doesn't have to be. Cricks can stay open all winter."

For a time they rode without speaking. Here and there a pool of water stood, but most of yesterday's rain had disappeared.

"What's it like when the river thaws?" Kate asked.

"Some years it just gets soft, like mush. Other years it goes out with a roar."

"And this year?" asked Kate.

"It's been warm," he said. "Warm weather melts the snow. Lots of rain makes it worse. All that water runs into the rivers upstream."

Kate moved restlessly, thinking about the heavy rain of the day before.

"Those rivers feed into the St. Croix," Anders went on. "The St. Croix gets higher and higher. As the water rises, it loosens the ice along the banks."

"And then?" Kate prodded.

"I've never seen it, but Papa says the current pushes the ice. It grinds and rumbles like thunder, and all of a sudden it goes out."

Kate's hands clenched. "And there's no place to get across."

"No place at all." Anders flicked the reins. Again he glanced at the sun, as though counting the minutes.

Before long, Kate pulled off the sweater Mama had knitted for her. It felt good to have such an unusually warm day in March. Yet Kate longed for food. "I'm hungry," she said.

"So am I. How would you like one of Mama's great big meals right now? Topped off with hot apple pie?"

"How do you think Mama is doing?" Kate asked.

"She'll be all right," Anders said quickly. He kept his gaze on the road as if he didn't want to talk about it.

But Kate wanted to know more. "Do you remember when Lars was born?"

"A little. I was only three and a half. I remember Tina more."

"What was it like?"

"When Tina was born? It was October. I was seven, almost eight."

"I mean, what happened?"

"Lars and I were the only ones home. Papa had taken a load of potatoes to Grantsburg. Tina came earlier than Papa and Mama expected."

Anders' voice softened. Only recently had he begun talking about his first mother. When he did, he always sounded—Kate wasn't sure she could describe it. Wistful, maybe? Sad at something that was gone forever?

"What did you do?"

"I ran to the nearest neighbor, the people who lived where Erik does now. I ran the whole way. When I got there, I couldn't breathe enough to tell them what was wrong. But Mrs. Sandquist took one look and knew. She grabbed her coat and a basket of things. By the time she came out of the house, Mr. Sandquist had the horses ready. I rode back with them."

"And when you got home?"

Anders laughed. "When we drove up in the yard, Lars came running out. 'Baby here!' he said. He looked real proud that he was the only one around to tell about it."

Anders pushed back his hair. "When we went inside, we heard a mighty squall. Mighty big for someone as small as Tina. Mama had taken care of everything."

"All by herself?"

"All by herself."

"She was all right?"

Anders nodded. "Mama was—" He paused, as if searching for words. "Well, you know how *your* Mama is."

"And yours," Kate answered softly, remembering what Mama had told him.

A tinge of red crept into Anders' cheeks, as though he remembered too. But he asked, "You know how your mama always tries to be strong?"

Kate giggled. "Yah," she drawled. "And how she brushes the tears away, as if it's wrong to let us see them."

"You betcha."

When they came to a steep hill, Anders slowed Wildfire. A narrow stream tumbled down next to the road. More water streamed over a bank of red earth. "Good clay for chinking logs," said Anders.

At the bottom of the hill he stopped the wagon. Walking back, he found the spring and called to Kate. "C'mon! Fill up on water!"

Cupping her hands, Kate caught the icy water, washed her face, and then drank. Her hunger didn't go away, but she felt better.

They continued on and soon saw a large log house ahead of them. "Must be Berglunds'," Anders said.

As they drove closer, they found it was a two-family house. According to Papa, Berglund and his family lived in one end, and Petersons in the other. Each end had its own kitchen with a chimney and a cellar underneath.

The large home sat at an angle on the edge of the hill. Nearby were two barns, one for each family. The haylofts were at ground level, instead of one story up. Alongside the barns, the hill dropped away.

Stopping Wildfire, Anders looped her lead rope around a rail. "Let's ask Berglunds for lunch."

"You can work for your meal," Kate teased. "The way you did at Johnson's."

As it turned out, no one answered their knock in either end of the house. Kate and Anders started down the hill, looking for someone. They found that cows lived in the lower level of each barn.

"When they get thirsty, they just stroll down to the river," Anders said.

In the side of the hill they discovered a cellar for storing cream, but no one was there. When they returned to the farmhouse, they climbed into the wagon, and took the trail to Tennessee Flats.

"According to Papa, we're almost there," Anders said.

"And we're ahead of time!" Kate could hardly believe her own words. "All we have to do is cross the ice, climb the hill, and wait for sundown."

As they passed into a flat field, Lutfisk ran off. Wildfire pricked her ears and moved more quickly.

From the high wagon seat, Kate looked west toward where the river should be. Beyond trees still bare of leaves, she caught a frightening glimpse.

A cold knot tightened her stomach. Quickly she glanced at Anders. Judging by the expression on his face, he, too, guessed the worst.

A moment later they came to a better view. Ahead of them stretched the blue waters of the St. Croix. The ice they needed for crossing the river was gone!

11

The Wild River

*W*ithout a word Anders urged Wildfire across the field to the landing known as Tennessee Flats. A worried frown lined his face.

As soon as they stopped, Kate dropped to the ground. Anders followed.

Around them lay great slabs of ice, thrown every which way, as though by a giant hand. Up and down the St. Croix, on both the Wisconsin and Minnesota sides, ice lined the shore.

Some of the great chunks stood on end, like jagged peaks pointing to the sky. Others lay almost flat, slanting only slightly.

Kate climbed onto one of those pieces. Stepping from one slab of ice to the next, she and Anders worked their way to the water.

"Has the ice just gone out?" Kate asked.

"Probably within the last day. Maybe even last night. Looks like we just missed crossing over."

The river was wide here—at least six or seven hundred feet across. The current was swift and strong with occasional chunks of ice floating downstream.

Kate stared at the deep blue water. As far as she could see in either direction, tall trees lined the hillsides.

"What a wild river!" she exclaimed. Yet she felt its beauty too.

Anders pointed at an opening in the trees across the river and downstream. "See that trail going off in the woods? That must be the landing. But the stone that marks it is covered by water."

To Kate it seemed as if her heart were being squeezed. If Ben came to the top of that hill, they wouldn't be able to see him. Nor would he be able to see them. Though the trees were still leafless from winter, their trunks and branches blocked the view.

Standing there, Kate felt the cold rising from the ice. She felt the wind across the water. Then, looking at the strong current, she felt hopeless.

"And this is supposed to be an easy crossing?"

"Yup," answered Anders. "It's wider here, but more shallow. In summer, I mean."

Kate sighed. "*Whatever* are we going to do?"

Anders shrugged, hunching his shoulders against the wind. "No ferries running yet. Little bit cold for swimming."

But the chill inside Kate came from more than ice. With all her heart she wanted to reach Ben before it was too late.

Like something burned into her mind, she remembered his words: "If you're there to meet me, I'll know you want to see me. If you're not, I'll go away and never trouble you again."

Anders still gazed across the river. "Wish I could have been here before loggers took out the big pine. Till then, this land didn't change in all the centuries the Chippewa Indians have been here."

Next to the crossing, Kate climbed off the ice. Here the ground eased down to the St. Croix with a gentle slope. Now in high water, the river bottom vanished almost immediately.

Going around the ice, Kate walked along the shore. *So I told Mama I'd help Anders figure out what to do,* she thought. Now the idea seemed ridiculous. Before they had left, Papa had prayed for courage, wisdom, and protection. They certainly needed that courage now.

The crossing was located at a bend in the river. Just upstream, stone piers anchored a boom of large logs linked together by chains. Once the river drive started, the boom would keep logs from piling up on shore.

Anders caught up to Kate. "I know one thing. We can't fight this current. We have to find a way to work with it."

"But how?" she asked. "Sand Creek was bad enough." Not by the biggest stretch of her imagination could she think of a way to work with the wild river.

She looked up at the sky. Judging by the sun, it had to be at least twelve o'clock. "Papa said we'd be in trouble. We sure are!"

Anders turned away from the river and started walking around. All of the snow was gone here, the ground dry. But farther back, under bushes and trees, the ground was soggy with long grass and wet leaves.

"What are you looking for?" Kate asked.

"People who use a crossing a lot sometimes leave a canoe or a boat. Maybe we can find one."

Anders and Kate headed in opposite directions. Starting upstream, Kate stopped at every clump of bushes. When she turned around and walked back, she noticed something she'd missed before. From the other direction it had seemed to be a log with branches and dead leaves over it.

This time Kate walked closer. Leaning down, she found the branches loose. When she pulled them away, she discovered a flat-bottomed rowboat. The boat lay upside down and was dirty and wet from being out all winter.

"Anders!" Kate shouted.

When she showed him her find, he looked excited. Together they tipped the boat over. The seams looked tight and the boat safe enough to use.

"That'll do it!" exclaimed Anders. "But there are no oars."

Again they searched, but this time without success. Even with oars, the trip across the swollen stream would be dangerous. They couldn't possibly navigate the river without them.

Then Kate remembered something. "You know, Anders, once Michael Reilly told me how he poled across a river."

"And who's Michael Reilly?" asked Anders.

"A boy I know."

"A boy you know," mimicked Anders. "Was this boy by any chance a friend?"

Kate felt a warm blush seep to the roots of her hair. Yes, of course, this boy was a friend when she lived in Minneapolis. Everyone in school knew that Michael was sweet on Kate. But she wouldn't tell Anders that.

"Michael said—"

Anders interrupted. "And Michael said—" His voice sounded high and sweet. "What, my dear sister, did Michael say?"

Kate flipped her long black braid over her shoulder. "If you will let me tell you," she said stiffly.

But Anders grinned. "You know, you might have the right idea—poling across, I mean. It's harder than oars, especially if I can't touch bottom. I've done it before, but not when the water ran this high."

Leaving the rowboat, he returned to the wagon. There he pulled out an ax and walked toward the trees farther up the shore.

As Kate trailed after him, her mind was far away. *Funny. I've almost forgotten about Michael. Maybe I'll go back to Minneapolis some time. Maybe I'll see him again.*

Kate knew that train fare would be an obstacle. Just the same, she didn't want to give up that hope.

Then her thoughts drifted to Erik. More than once he'd been a real friend. Kate liked talking to him and liked the kind of person he was. *I wonder who I'll marry when I grow up.*

Anders soon found a dead branch that was the size he needed. Using the ax, he shaped a pole about eight feet long and two inches thick.

When he returned to the crossing, he unhitched Wildfire from the wagon. Slipping on her halter, he led her to a patch of meadow grass and tied her lead rope to a stake. Then he and Kate dragged the rowboat down to the river crossing.

Lutfisk leaped into the front of the boat. With his tongue hanging out, he seemed to laugh at his master.

"All right, all right," Anders said. "You get to go along."

Lutfisk flopped on his belly between the first and second seats.

When Kate climbed into the boat, she reached down and slipped her fingers into the river. Quickly she pulled them out. Even close to shore, the water sent a cold tingle up her arm.

"You're sure we can make it across?" she asked. The rowboat seemed smaller all the time, and the river wider and deeper. Both of them were good swimmers, but Kate knew they wouldn't last long in the icy water.

As Anders gazed across the river, he seemed just as uneasy. "Current's mighty strong out there. It's deep, even here where it should be shallow."

"What if we get out in the middle, and you can't touch bottom with the pole?" Kate asked.

"That's what bothers me. The current will take us wherever it wants to go."

"Anders," Kate said slowly, as an idea came to her. "I just remembered something else."

She spoke quickly before Anders could tease her again. "You know, that story I heard about poling across the river? First Michael went upstream, along the shore, where he could touch bottom with the pole."

Anders grinned, as though he already guessed what she'd say. "Then he shoved out into the current, and it carried him downstream. Yup, you've got it, Kate."

As Anders pushed off from shore, the boat grated on gravel. When he stepped in, it rocked beneath his weight.

Bracing his feet squarely, Anders stood up. Pushing with the pole, he sent the boat upstream. Kate faced the bow and watched for rocks.

At first they followed the shoreline where it was more shallow. There the water lapped gently against the sides of the boat. Sunlight danced across the ripples on the water. But a few feet farther out, the current ran deep and strong.

Before long, Anders pulled off his jacket. Each time he used the pole, his muscles rippled beneath his cotton shirt.

Soon he found a rhythm, and they started making good time.

As they came into a small bay in the river, Kate saw animals playing on the ice.

With short legs and long bodies, they had black velvet-like paws and dark brown fur. Their thick muscular tails tapered down to a tip.

Kate turned back to Anders. "Are they otters?" she whispered and reached down to hold Lutfisk quiet. Kate had heard about otters, but had never seen them.

Anders grinned and nodded. Digging the pole into the river bottom, he held the boat from slipping downstream.

The otters had found a huge slab of ice next to the river. As Kate and Anders watched, one of the otters took three or four leaps and jumped. With forelegs back, it slid ten or twelve feet on its belly. Across the ice and down the muddy bank it went, then into the water.

Soon another otter followed the first. Already they had made a slide in the mud with a six-inch-wide groove.

Were they fishing or playing? Kate wasn't sure. The otters swam with heads high, well out of the water, and their backs slightly exposed.

Before long, a large otter turned toward the boat and hissed and snorted. Kate and Anders remained still. When the otter seemed satisfied that they weren't a threat, it went back to the others.

As Kate watched the animals play, all the discouragements of the day fell away. Then Anders started poling again. Soon they left the bay behind and continued up the swollen river.

"Hang on now," he said at last. "It's a mighty wobbly boat. And you lie still, Lutfisk."

With a big shove, Anders pushed away from shore. As the current caught the flat-bottomed boat, Kate clutched the sides.

Each time Anders dipped the pole, they moved farther out into the river. When he could no longer touch bottom, he sat down. Faster and faster they moved with the current sending them downstream.

Just then Kate heard the hooting of an owl. She turned her head to listen. From far away the lonely cry came.

For some reason the call made Kate uneasy. "Anders, is that an owl?"

Without thinking, she twisted around. The boat rocked with her sudden movement.

"Kate!" Anders shouted.

Kate's heart flip-flopped as water splashed over the side of the boat. It rocked again, and she hung on with all her strength.

Then, still quivering, the little boat settled once more into the current.

Kate no longer heard the call, but this time she faced ahead instead of turning. "Was it an owl?"

"Yup," answered her brother. "A barred owl. Or a mighty good imitation."

"In broad daylight?" Kate asked. "Are you sure it's an owl?" She remembered Erik on the way to the maple-syrup making. "Have you ever heard an owl during the day?"

"Yah sure. Once when Erik and I were out in the woods, he started calling like a crow."

Anders laughed. "An owl got mad and kept answering back. I walked till I was almost up to him. He had brownish-gray bars right across his breast. Saw him perched on a branch, as big as you please. When I got too close, he flew away. Have you ever seen one of those big ones fly between trees?"

Kate shook her head.

"Their wings are so wide, I can't figure out how they miss the branches."

As a large chunk of ice floated near, Anders used the pole to push it away. Then Kate heard a faraway sound. What was it? A human voice? She wasn't sure.

This time she turned slowly to avoid rocking the boat. Looking back, she scanned the shore on the Wisconsin side of the river. Someone was there, standing on a slab of ice.

"Anders! It's Joe! He's trying to tell us something!"

As Anders started to look around, the current caught the flat-bottomed boat and thrust it into rapids. The boat moved faster and faster.

"We're in trouble," Anders said suddenly, his voice tense.

Kate clutched the sides of the boat. Then she saw what he meant.

The high water was bad enough. The rapids swirling around them were even worse. But now, huge logs were coming downstream.

"The river drive has started!" said Anders.

Kate's hands tightened with fear. What if one of the logs crashed into them?

In the next instant the little boat hit an eddy and spun.

12

Another Warning

"Don't move," Anders warned Kate. "Stay, Lutfisk," he ordered when the dog started to stand up.

The boat leaned to one side, spun again, and straightened.

Kate drew a deep breath, but they weren't out of danger yet. Only two feet away a huge log bore down upon them.

"Hang on," said Anders. "No matter what happens, don't let go of the boat." Grasping his long pole, he pushed against the log until it floated past them.

A moment later another log threatened them. Again Anders pushed it off. But a third log struck them broadside.

As the small boat rocked, water sloshed into the bottom. Filled with panic, Kate clung to the sides until her knuckles turned white. Then the boat moved with the log and was not damaged.

Anders reached out with his pole. With a mighty thrust, he shoved the huge log away.

As it slid past them, Kate straightened her shoulders. Yet fear still washed over her, as cold as the water around them.

Anders lowered the pole into the river but could not touch bottom. Twice more the logs came too fast, thudding against the boat. Each time it shuddered with the impact. Each time Anders pushed the logs aside.

When Kate finally dared look toward shore, the current had carried them downstream. "Joe wants us to come back," she told Anders.

Her brother groaned. "You're sure?"

As Kate watched, Joe raised his arm and motioned for them to come his way.

"Can't think of anything I want to do less," Anders grumbled. "But it must be something important."

He dipped the pole into the river. Though it didn't grab water like an oar, the pole turned the boat just enough. The current took them toward the Wisconsin shore.

When at last the pole touched bottom, Anders braced his feet and stood up. They'd gone beyond the landing at Tennessee Flats, but Joe kept up with them along the riverbank.

As they came to an island, Anders eased the boat into a quiet channel. Ahead of them, a sandstone cliff rose from the water. Anders landed the boat where the bank was still low.

Joe caught the bow. "Your father asked me to find you," he said to Anders. "After you left, another letter came from Bernhard."

Joe looked at Kate. "Your mother's brother?"

"Ben," she said, as she climbed out of the boat.

"Ben," repeated Joe. "In his letter he said, 'After I wrote, I met a man from your area. He told me that if the ice went out, no one could cross at Tennessee Flats.' "

Anders laughed. "Well, at least he's got *that* right!"

As the boys pulled the boat farther up the bank, Joe kept talking. "Ben said, 'If you want to see me, I'll be at the Rush City ferry landing instead.' "

"The ferry!" Anders looked as if he couldn't believe the bad news. "Lot of good that will do!" He pushed his blond hair out of his eyes. "The ferry's not running yet. Because it's held by cables, a log could smash a hole right through its side."

"I know," answered Joe. "But Ben will be on the Minnesota side at sundown today."

"Today!" Kate exclaimed. The sun was past the midpoint. It beat down upon them, giving unusual warmth for this time of the year. Was it one o'clock? Two o'clock?

Kate wasn't sure, but she did know one thing. "We haven't got much time!"

Anders groaned. "Let me tell you the rest. Ben also said, 'If you're not there, I'll believe you don't want to see me. I'll go away and never bother you again.' "

Joe's black eyes danced. "Yah sure, you betcha."

Kate giggled, and Anders grinned. Yet before long he looked back at the main channel of the river. By now, logs floated past in a steady stream, filling the water from the Wisconsin to the Minnesota side.

"Worst of all, I'm hungry," said Anders. "We left our food in Sand Creek."

"I'll get some for you," Joe answered. He pulled a coil of flexible wire from his pocket. "I'll set a snare."

At the thought of food, Kate felt famished again. Yet she also felt grateful that Joe had reached them in time.

"If we'd gone up the hill, we would have missed you," she said. "How did you find us?"

"I followed your tracks. It wasn't hard. You make big ones." He grinned. "Not you, Kate. Anders and Wildfire."

The two boys picked up the boat. Carrying it between them, they walked back to the landing at Tennessee Flats.

"I don't know the way to the Rush City ferry," Anders said. "How far is it?"

Joe thought for a moment. "On the road, maybe seventeen, eighteen miles."

Kate gasped. "That's farther than from home to Grantsburg."

"There's no road that goes straight through," Joe said. "If you take the wagon, you'll have a long trip around. I'll show you a shorter way."

When Wildfire saw them coming, she tossed her head and whinnied. The boys returned the rowboat to its place near the landing. Then Joe picked up a stick and drew a map in the sand.

"There's an old Indian trail starting here at Tennessee Flats.

It goes across this field, through a swamp, and up over that hill."

He pointed, then lengthened the line. "Here's where you cross Wood River."

"We don't have any choice?" Kate felt nervous just thinking about it.

"There's no bridge except at Grantsburg," Anders reminded her. "If we go back to town, it'll be an extra ten or eleven miles. We don't have enough time."

Kate sighed. The Wood River was narrower than the St. Croix. Yet if farmers opened the dam and let water out of Big Wood Lake, Wood River would run deep and swift. There'd also be logs coming down.

Again Joe drew a line. "After you cross Wood River, keep going this way. At Fish Lake School, there's a path through the woods. It angles south to Steven Powell's farm on the St. Croix. From there keep on till you get to the ferry landing."

Kate studied the map. It looked like one long, almost straight line running roughly parallel with the St. Croix River.

Kate took the bucket to get water from the river for Wildfire. On the way back, she saw the two boys talking. When Anders looked her way, he suddenly stopped.

It made Kate feel uncomfortable. Yet it wasn't hard to guess what he and Joe were saying. Once she and Anders reached the ferry landing, they'd have to cross the St. Croix again. With the log drive started, that seemed even more impossible.

Anders left the halter under Wildfire's bridle and tied the lead rope around his waist. Coiling the long reins, he tied up the slack.

"The trail's not wide enough for a wagon," he told Kate. "So don't bring anything you can leave behind."

They left their coats in the wagon, and took only their sweaters. Anders put the match tin in his shirt pocket and buckled a hatchet inside a holder on his belt. After jumping onto Wildfire's back, he helped Kate up behind him.

As Anders lifted the reins, Joe stood back from the horse.

"There's someone in the woods," he warned. "Someone who doesn't belong there, I mean."

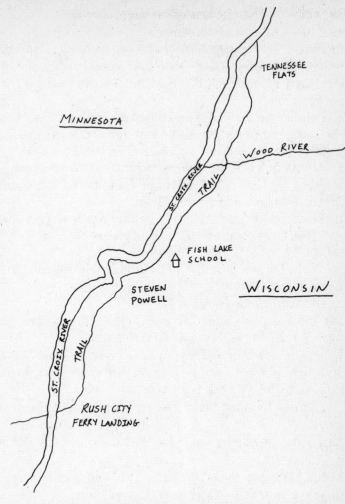

Though ready to flick the reins, Anders stopped. His hands seemed frozen in midair.

"It's a man with big feet, big boots," Joe went on. "He followed you. He walked all around the place where you built a fire."

"And the place where I found the cow?" Kate felt uneasy, remembering that she'd been alone.

Joe nodded. "Then he started coming this way."

"After us?" Kate barely breathed.

"After you for a while." Joe's black eyes no longer danced.

"Maybe that's what I saw," Kate said slowly. "Someone on a horse seemed to slip behind a tree. But I wasn't sure if I was imagining things."

"Sometimes he walked. Sometimes he rode a horse. Every once in a while he pulled his horse into the woods. At one place the ground was marked up, as if he waited there for a bit."

"You think he's still somewhere behind us?" Anders asked.

Joe shook his head. "Not anymore. He followed you a ways, then headed down toward Wood River."

He pointed at the map. "He's not behind you now. He's ahead of you." Tossing away the stick, he rubbed out the map with his moccasin.

In spite of the warm sun, Kate suddenly felt chilled. "So we might run right into him."

Joe nodded, his face solemn.

Kate tried to push aside her uneasiness. "Maybe he's gone by now." Yet she knew it was wishful thinking.

"Or maybe he's waiting for you, Kate!" said Anders. "Maybe he'll hide behind a bush and pounce on you when you ride past! Maybe he'll snatch you off, right behind my back!"

Kate flipped her long braid over her shoulder. "Anders, you are mean!"

Her brother winked toward Joe. But the other boy did not smile.

"Listen to my warning," he said. "The man is evil."

Anders' grin faded. "Evil? How do you know?"

"When I was in Grantsburg, I heard there's been a couple of men hanging around town—men that people don't know. Both are tall, but not fat. One of them has a small scar on the center of his chin."

Kate's fingers clenched. She looked at her brother's back and wished she knew what he was thinking. Was Anders also remembering the scar on Ben's chin?

"Do you know which of the men was following us?" Anders asked.

Joe shrugged. "I saw only one of them, and it was almost dark. He was watching people along the street, staring at them like—"

Joe paused as though words failed him.

"Like his eyes were cold," Kate said.

Joe nodded, but Anders laughed. "So we have an evil man with cold eyes!"

In spite of his teasing, Kate remembered how she felt when she saw the stranger. "Joe, can you go with us?" she asked quickly.

He nodded. "I'll come with you till I hear a partridge drumming. Then I'll get food and catch up again."

"If you're off somewhere, is there some way we can signal you? If we need help, I mean?"

"Call me," he said. "Call me with the hooting of an owl."

13

Fight for Life

*K*ate stared at Joe. That night in the woods Erik had insisted that what they'd heard wasn't a real owl. Only a short time ago, when they were out on the river, she'd heard the hooting again.

"Joe?" asked Kate. "Do you practice calling like an owl?"

When he grinned, Kate had her answer. "Will you show us how?" she asked.

In answer he gave the call of a barred owl. *Whoo, whoo, whoo, whoo—whoo, whoo, whoo, whoo-ah!*

It gave Kate a strange feeling. Joe stood directly in front of her, yet the hooting sounded as real as what she'd heard in the woods.

"Want to try it?" Joe asked. "The call of an owl is the Chippewa word for owl. We say, *goo-coo-ka-oo*."

Kate listened closely. Sure enough, when she used the Chippewa words Joe told her, it sounded like the hooting she'd heard. He'd added only a few words to imitate a barred owl.

Several times Kate tried the call, and finally Joe said, "That's it. I'll hoot like a barred owl three times to tell you where I am. You call back, and we'll find each other."

"And if there's danger?" Kate asked.

"I'll change the call with the *whoo-ah!* fourth, instead of at the end. You'll know it's not a real owl."

Anders flicked the reins, and Wildfire started across the field with Kate riding behind Anders. Joe ran alongside, and Lutfisk followed him.

When they reached the swamp, Joe ran ahead. The narrow path took the high spots through marshy areas, then brought them up a steep hill. When they came out on a ridge, Joe left them to hunt for food.

Anders turned to Kate. "If we spot the timber swindler, we'll sneak away so he doesn't see us. We'll head for Grantsburg and Big Gust." His voice sounded confident, as though he could handle anything.

"You're mighty sure of yourself," Kate said.

"Yup. If we find the swindler, we won't *let* him hurt us."

"But Joe says he's big. And remember? The man we saw near Wood Lake was big. Tall, I mean."

"Tall doesn't always mean strong." Anders flexed his muscles. "'Course with me, it does."

Kate did not smile. She knew that with each step Wildfire took, they were riding into danger.

As they followed the old Indian trail, the woods grew close. Jack pine with sharply pointed needles reached out, brushing against Kate's arms and legs. More than once she jumped before she realized it was only a branch.

"I'm hungry," Anders said after a while. "Really hungry."

"My stomach's growling," Kate answered.

"You don't have to tell me. I can hear it."

By now the skin on Kate's face felt tight and drawn, as though sunburned. She rubbed her nose, and it hurt.

For a time they rode along the ridge. After several turns in the trail, Kate felt uneasy. Joe hadn't said anything about these turns. Had he shown them just the general direction they should take?

Finally Anders pulled up Wildfire. "Do you think we're headed the right way?"

Kate knew her brother well enough to guess that he was trying to hide his worry. She remembered Joe's map. "We should be getting close to Wood River."

As she spoke, both of them glanced up at the sky. A stand of jack pine made it impossible to see the sun. Without the sun they could not tell either time or direction. Except for the thin, packed-down line of the trail ahead, there was no break in the trees.

"Mighty lonely out here," Anders said lightly.

"Mighty creepy, you mean." The pine and oak closed in around Kate, giving her the feeling of a nighttime woods.

Her brother clucked to Wildfire, and the mare stepped out.

"Anders," Kate said, as she tried to take her mind off the eerie woods. "What do you think is happening to Mama?"

When he didn't answer, Kate asked again, "What if she's having the baby right at this moment? What if she's having it, and we don't even know?"

Anders shrugged, and Kate wished she could see his eyes. She felt sure he cared, more than he would say.

"Do you think she's all right?"

"I think she's all right." But his voice lacked his usual confidence.

Kate looked around. *I don't like these woods*, she thought again. There was something about the way the trees closed in. She couldn't explain it. It was something she felt.

Silly! She tried to laugh at herself, but then she wondered: Was it really the forest that bothered her, or something more? Maybe Joe was right—that an evil man walked in these woods.

"Where's Lutfisk?" Kate asked, when she realized she hadn't seen him for some time.

"He always comes back," Anders told her. "He'll find us."

A moment later Kate heard a strange sound. It reminded her of the night near Wood Lake. She poked Anders in the back.

Her brother pulled up Wildfire. As the mare came to a halt, Kate heard the noise more clearly. It was sawing, all right, and close at hand.

Anders slipped down from Wildfire and tied her lead rope

to a tree. Quietly Kate followed her brother.

With each step they took, the sawing grew more distinct. Then as Kate listened, it stopped.

Careful to avoid any branch that would snap, they came at last to an opening in the trees. A large pile of logs stood on the banks of what had to be the Wood River.

Without making a sound, they crept forward. Then Anders put a warning hand on Kate's arm. His lips shaped a word: Wait.

Wait for what? Kate wanted to see the timber swindler, to know who he was.

Anders' frown held her back. When she stopped, he headed for the clearing. Each time he came to another tree, he stood behind it, looking ahead. Then, step by step, he moved on.

When Anders reached the end of the large pile of logs, he looked around and motioned for Kate to come. As she caught up to him, he pointed to a battered black hat on top of the logs.

On the ground lay sawdust and thin slices of wood—pieces of wood newly sawed from the end of the logs. The timber swindler had to be nearby.

Kate's hands knotted into fists. "Where is he?" she whispered. In the stillness her words seemed loud to her ears.

Anders stepped forward into the sawdust. Picking up a small slice of wood with a brand on it, he slipped it inside his shirt.

Then Kate noticed his tracks. In the soft earth near the riverbank, as well as in the sawdust, her brother's boot prints showed clearly.

Kate pointed down. Scuffling his feet, Anders tried to hide his tracks. In that moment Kate heard the sharp crack of someone stepping on a dry branch.

"Anders!" Kate warned hoarsely.

Her brother turned his head toward the sound, and both of them listened. Whoever it was seemed to think he was all alone in the woods.

"The swindler is coming back!" Kate whispered.

Anders bounded away from the pile of logs. Kate followed him into a tangle of underbrush. For a moment they knelt down behind a clump of bushes.

The bare, leafless branches offered little shelter, but from here Kate could see the timber swindler. Tall and fairly slender, he walked to the pile of logs with quick, sure movements. As he started sawing, he stood with his back toward them.

"I want to see his face," Anders said in a low voice. "Let's go around on the other side."

"You mean, let's get out of here," whispered Kate. "It would be much smarter to leave."

Before they could slip into the woods, a dog barked from somewhere off in the trees.

"Lutfisk!" whispered Anders.

The swindler raised his head, listened, and dropped his saw. As he picked up his branding hammer, he looked at the ground.

Anders groaned. "He sees my tracks."

A moment later, Lutfisk barked again. This time he sounded closer.

"He'll give us away," Kate said.

Crouching almost double, Anders crept deeper into the woods, followed by Kate. Moving from tree to tree, they circled the clearing. When they found the trail, they started running.

By the time they came to Wildfire, Kate was out of breath. Anders untied the mare's rope and jumped on her back. Reaching down, he pulled Kate up behind him, then urged Wildfire ahead.

At a turn in the trail, Lutfisk found them. Kate glanced back. No one followed behind.

"We got away," she whispered, still afraid to speak aloud.

"Not yet," Anders warned.

Their path wound around the place where the swindler worked. Knowing that he would pick up any sound, Anders kept Wildfire to a walk. Before long, the trail brought them to another part of the Wood River.

Again Kate looked around. She couldn't push aside her worry that the man would follow. So far the road was empty.

Then Wildfire started down the steep hill. Kate and Anders leaned back to help the mare keep her footing. The trail behind them slipped out of sight.

The Wood River twisted and turned between large trees as it found its way to the St. Croix. Swollen by rain and melting snow, the usually narrow river flowed beyond its banks.

Anders studied the swiftly moving water. "An old-timer would drop a tree for a bridge," he told Kate. "But we don't have the time or the saw. You'll have to go over on Wildfire's back."

Filled with dread, Kate gazed at the cold, dark water. Lately she'd ridden the mare often, but taking her across a flooded river was another matter.

"What about you?" she asked. "Wildfire can carry both of us."

"Don't want to take a chance on our weight. She'll probably have to swim for it."

"So what are you going to do?"

Anders offered his lopsided grin. "Me? I'm riding that log."

He tipped his head toward the bank. About five feet above the waterline, two small slender trees kept an old log from rolling into the river.

"Are you serious?" Kate asked.

"Yup. Used to practice on Rice Lake. If I ever work on a river drive, I'll have to know how."

"You'll have to know how, all right. The water will be mighty cold if you fall!"

"You haven't seen log drivers compete against one another. They can stand and run on a log all day." Anders pulled off his boots and tied them inside his sweater.

"Give me yours," he said to Kate.

She stepped back. "If you get dunked, you'll lose 'em."

"No, I won't. But they *will* get wet when *you* ride across."

Kate found that hard to believe. Surely she'd stay drier on Wildfire than he would standing on a log.

"Hurry," said Anders as he rolled up his pant legs. "The swindler might catch up any minute. And we've got to find Ben."

Though still unwilling, Kate yanked off her boots and stockings and tied them inside her sweater.

Going over to the log, Anders worked it free from the trees. Then he knotted both his sweater and Kate's around his neck.

Returning to Wildfire, he took hold of the bridle. With Kate on the mare's back, Anders led the horse to the water. Wildfire snorted and stepped away.

Anders tugged at her bridle. The mare started to rear. Kate slid back and almost fell off.

Her brother spoke sharply, and Wildfire settled down, but her eyes rolled with fear. Anders waited a minute, then let go of the bridle.

Kate tightened the reins. The mare moved restlessly, as though sensing Kate's panic.

"If she starts to swim, grab her mane and slide back on her," Anders said as he started toward the log. "If you lean forward you'll push her head down. You have to keep her nose out of water."

Trying to act brave, Kate patted the mare's neck. "It's all right, girl. You haven't got a wagon this time."

Wildfire turned her ears to the sound of Kate's voice, but stood her place. With butterflies churning her stomach, Kate clucked to the mare.

"Dig in your heels," called Anders softly from near the log. "You have to let her know who's boss."

Again Kate urged Wildfire ahead, but the mare refused to obey.

"She'll come when I shove out," said Anders. "If I float downstream, try to take her straight across."

Anders rolled the log the rest of the way down the bank. When it tumbled into the water, he jumped on.

The log rocked, then spun, and Anders nearly lost his balance. With waving arms he faced into the spin. His feet moved quickly, as though he were running in place.

By the time the log slowed its spinning, Anders was halfway across the river. He looked toward Kate and grinned, then called to Lutfisk.

The dog jumped into the water and paddled toward Anders. But Wildfire stayed on the bank, still afraid to go on.

Kate gritted her teeth. *I can do anything my brother can do,* she told herself. Again she dug in her heels. But the mare did not move.

Anders whistled. Immediately the mare responded. As she plunged into the river, the icy water touched Kate's bare feet.

"Yowie!" she cried out, in spite of her best intentions.

Anders grinned. In the next instant, the log beneath his feet rolled in the opposite direction. His arms thrashed the air. Then he turned into the spin and ran in place.

Wildfire whinnied, and Kate clucked to her. "Go to Anders." The river reached Kate's knees, and she flinched against the cold.

Then the water came level with the mare's back, and Kate realized that Wildfire was swimming. Clutching her mane, Kate slid back on the horse.

As the water crept through her clothes, panic washed through Kate. For the first time she wondered if she could hang on.

"Anders!" she called. No longer did she care if she kept up to him. No longer did it matter what he thought. She wanted only to live.

But Anders had landed downstream on the far bank. As though from far away, Kate heard his call, "C'mon, Wildfire." Again he whistled.

Then the current caught Kate, sweeping her off the mare's back. In water over her head, Kate clung to the mane, frozen by a terror colder than the river.

14

Which Way Now?

A moment later Wildfire touched bottom and stood up. As the mare climbed onto the bank, Kate staggered with her to solid ground.

When Anders reached them, he took hold of the bridle. "Good girl!" he said. "I'm proud of you."

Surprised by the unusual praise, Kate turned toward Anders. But he wasn't talking to her.

The mare nudged the boy's shoulder, as though agreeing with him. When she shook herself, beads of water flew off her back in every direction.

The air that seemed warm before the river crossing left Kate shaking. "I need a fire," she said.

As Anders pulled on his boots, he glanced across the river. "I don't dare make one." He gave Kate both sweaters, but told her, "Take only a minute. The swindler probably heard our noise."

Behind a clump of bushes, Kate wrung out her skirt. With hands fumbling with cold, she shrugged into her sweater. Her long stockings proved even more difficult. When she tried to pull them on, they clung to her wet skin.

She struggled with her boots next. Wondering if she'd ever be warm again, she put her brother's sweater over her own.

"Hurry up!" Anders called softly.

When Kate returned to him, Anders was keeping watch, looking back across the river.

"Have you seen anything?" she asked through chattering teeth.

Her brother shook his head. "But the swindler will come. If he followed us before with no reason—"

"No reason?" Kate asked. "We saw him at Wood Lake, don't forget! Remember what you said? 'If we see the timber swindler, we'll just sneak away and get Big Gust!' "

Anders only laughed. "That's what we'll do, all right."

"But what will the swindler do if he finds *us*?" Kate asked.

Anders shrugged, but his eyes were more serious than usual. "Probably hide us somewhere to make sure we don't tell anyone what he's doing. At least not till he's collected the money from the sawmill."

Kate trembled. The chill she felt came from more than cold water.

With a bound Anders leaped onto Wildfire. Reaching down a hand, he pulled Kate up behind him, then flicked the reins.

"Did the swindler have a horse?" Kate asked as they started out.

"Yup. Standing off to one side. A good looking bay with long slender legs. Bet she can run fast."

For a time they rode at a steady pace. As the air struck Kate's wet hair and skirt, she shivered till she thought she'd fall off. Yet she couldn't ask Anders to stop.

When they neared a bend in the road, Kate looked back.

"Anders!" she exclaimed, her voice tense.

A man had ridden up behind them. Though still some distance away, he was riding hard, closing the gap.

As Anders twisted around, Kate pointed.

The man's black hat hid his face, but she had no doubt about the bay horse. Its long legs reached out, seeming to fly over the dirt road.

"Hold on!" exclaimed Anders, and Kate grabbed him around the middle. He dug in his heels and slapped the reins at the same time. Wildfire bolted forward.

The pounding gallop tore at Kate's insides. Just as she felt she could handle it no longer, Anders slowed the mare and turned his head.

"We have to get away from the road. If we stay here, it's just a test of who runs fastest."

Kate didn't like that idea one bit. Wildfire had been traveling hard much of the day. A fresh horse would have the advantage.

"Help me find a place," Anders said. "We've got to hide."

About fifteen yards farther on, Kate pointed to a gap in the underbrush along the side of the road. Anders turned Wildfire into the bushes.

The opening was barely wide enough for a horse to pass through. As soon as jack pine screened them from view, Kate and Anders slid down.

Quickly he snapped on the mare's lead rope. "Take Wildfire in as far as you can. I'll get rid of the hoof prints."

Grabbing a pine branch from the ground, Anders headed back to the road.

As Kate hurried the mare deeper into the woods, Lutfisk caught up. He was wet and covered with sand, and his long tongue hung out.

When Anders found them again, he'd been running hard. "I went back as far as I dared," he said when he caught his breath. "The swindler will figure out that we left the road. But if he follows from where our tracks leave off, he'll enter the woods at a different place."

Anders took the lead rope from Kate. "Be quiet," he warned. "The swindler can't be far behind."

Before long, distant hoofbeats sounded along the road. Anders stopped and put his hand across Wildfire's muzzle.

"Get Lutfisk," he whispered to Kate.

Quickly Kate knelt down. As she tried to keep the dog quiet, the hoofbeats moved nearer. Closer and closer the horse came.

Kate's hands tightened. What if Lutfisk barked? Or Wildfire whinnied?

Soon the horse came even with the trees where they stood. The moment seemed to last forever.

Then the hoofbeats passed beyond them and faded away.

Kate sat back. For a few minutes, at least, they were safe. But her heart still pounded.

As they started out again through the woods, Anders walked at a rapid pace, leading Wildfire. Lutfisk darted in and out of the trees.

Ducking beneath low-hanging branches, Anders picked his way between the jack pine and oak. Often Kate needed to take running steps to keep up with his longer stride.

The faster Anders moved, the more afraid Kate became. What if she lost sight of him? All she could think about was the man on the road. When would he turn and come back?

By the time they'd gone some distance, Kate's side ached with hurrying. Whenever the pines allowed a view of the sky, she looked up. *It's a good thing Anders knows where we're going.* She felt more and more confused.

Sometimes they seemed to head south, other times west, and occasionally, even a bit north. But Kate staggered on, following her tall brother.

When he finally slowed his headlong pace, she whispered, "How will Joe find us?"

"No problem," said Anders. "Joe can track anybody or anything."

"But if he can find us, so can the swindler."

"Depends on how good a tracker he is. He might be fooled by the brush marks. Joe won't be. He'll just follow the marks into the trees."

"I wish Joe would catch up," Kate said.

Anders hurried around any soft ground where they might leave footprints. At last they came to a spring and a clearing where it was safe to build a fire.

There Anders stopped and let the reins trail. Wildfire nosed the ground for grass.

"Take a minute," Anders said in a quiet voice, and his kindness surprised Kate.

Feeling grateful for a chance to rest, she dropped down on a log. During their race through the woods, she'd grown warmer. But now when they stopped, she trembled again.

Quickly her brother collected dry leaves and small branches. In a sheltered spot he started a fire with one of their two remaining matches. Gradually he added the driest wood he could find in the hope that smoke wouldn't betray them.

Unbraiding her long hair, Kate shook it out, then crept closer to the small fire. Lutfisk perked his ears and tipped his head from side to side.

"You crazy dog," she said, petting him in spite of his wetness. While they faced endless trouble, Lutfisk looked as if he were having the time of his life.

As Kate grew warmer, her shivering finally stopped. Yet worry felt like a weight on her back.

"Anders?" she asked, as he sat down next to her. Kate spoke softly to make sure she wouldn't be heard. "If Ben is the timber swindler—"

She paused, afraid to go on. Still it was something she had to know.

"If Ben is the swindler, he needs to reach the St. Croix ahead of us, doesn't he?"

" 'Fraid so, Kate." Her brother's voice was little more than a whisper.

"I keep thinking about Mama. I think about the way she looks at that picture."

"The one of her family?"

Kate nodded. "If we find Ben, how will we know if we can trust him?"

Anders shrugged. "We don't know that he's the swindler."

"I'm scared about taking Ben home to Mama," Kate answered. "How will she feel if he's still lying and stealing?"

"Don't worry your head about it," Anders said.

"But I do." Kate looked up into his eyes. "How can Mama forgive Ben when she might lose so much? She's taking a big chance about whether he's honest."

When Anders didn't reply, Kate kept thinking about it. Then suddenly, as though a candle were lit, she felt sure of something. *Mama forgives Ben because Jesus forgave her!*

The idea startled Kate. Through his death on the cross, Jesus had provided a way for anyone who felt sorry and asked forgiveness to be forgiven. By inviting Ben home, Mama was offering that kind of forgiveness.

It made Kate feel proud of her mother. At the same time, she didn't want Mama hurt even more.

"Anders," Kate said quietly. "Wouldn't it be awful to have your brother betray you?"

Anders grinned. "Or your sister."

"Anders, I'm serious. Wouldn't it be terrible? Someone from your own family, and you couldn't trust him?"

"Well, you know how it is," Anders said lightly. "Everybody has a sister they can't trust."

Kate stared at him. "What do I have to do to get you to understand? I'm really scared! All you do is make a joke of it."

Anders looked her straight in the eye. For once no laughter played around his face. "Kate, there's one thing I promise you. Even though I tease you, you can trust me."

Without warning, tears blurred Kate's vision. Impatiently she brushed them away. Yet even that reminded her of Mama.

"Thanks, Anders," Kate said, her voice softer than it needed to be.

Anders looked down at his feet, as though her tears made him nervous. Something inside Kate trembled and broke.

Strange, she thought. *I'm not mad at Anders anymore. I want to trust him, like Mama wants to trust Ben.*

Is that what forgiveness is? Going beyond the bad times? Accepting a brother just the way he is?

"Thanks," Kate said again. She felt amazed that her brother seemed to understand.

Anders grinned. "Think nothing of it. Every now and then I have to remind you what a fine fellow I am."

But Kate wasn't fooled. She knew that he really cared about

what happened to Mama and Ben. He even seemed to care about what happened to her.

"We have to get moving," Anders said after a moment. "Or we'll never find Mama's little brother."

Kate was starting to warm up, but she knew they couldn't wait long enough for her skirt to dry. Quickly she pulled back her hair and braided it again.

Anders bent a piece of birchbark into a container. Bringing water from the spring, he put out the fire.

Kate walked to an opening in the trees. Between the branches of an oak, she found the sun. "Something isn't right," she said.

Then she knew what it was. "We're going the wrong way."

Anders stared at her. "You're sure?"

Kate nodded. She felt as though she were staring into a bottomless pit.

Coming to where she stood, Anders studied the sky and groaned. "We got turned around. Probably when we were moving so fast."

"We've been going back to Wood River, haven't we?" asked Kate.

"'Fraid so." Anders sounded sick. "And the sun's getting lower all the time."

15

Caught Between!

*W*ith a look of panic in his eyes, Anders led Wildfire to a nearby stump. Kate climbed onto the mare's back. Using the lead rope, Anders hurried ahead of his horse.

Faster and faster they moved. Whenever they reached an open place in the trees, Anders looked up. Whenever he looked up, he increased his pace. But the worried look didn't leave his eyes. Kate knew he wasn't really sure where he was going.

Ducking low-hanging branches, Kate tightened nervous fingers in Wildfire's mane.

"What if Ben leaves before we get there?" she asked. The thought haunted her. "He'll go away, thinking we don't care."

Anders glanced back as if he'd heard her. Yet he didn't answer. Even his eyes looked discouraged.

"Anders?" Kate asked.

When her brother still ignored her, Kate raised her voice. "Anders!"

This time he turned to her. "Shhhhh!"

Kate reached forward and tugged the lead rope. Her brother had to stop.

"Anders," she said. "We'll never make it."

"I know. It's impossible." For the first time Anders seemed to give up hope. "We've tried everything!"

"No, we haven't," Kate answered. "Before we left, Papa prayed for us. He asked God to give us wisdom—to help us know what we needed to do. But *we* haven't asked God for help."

She remembered her panic-filled prayer when Anders disappeared in Sand Creek. "We haven't asked God together, I mean."

Anders looked at her, and Kate saw the struggle in his face. Then he said, "Well, at home Papa always prays. So I guess I should try."

He looked uncomfortable, as though hoping Kate wouldn't make a smart remark. She felt too surprised to think of one. Instead, she bowed her head.

For a moment Anders stood without speaking, as if wondering what to ask. "We give up, God," he said finally. "We don't know what to do."

Again he paused, then prayed, "Will you show us where we are? And Jesus, if Ben is honest, help us reach him in time."

"Ah-men," Kate said.

When she opened her eyes, both she and Anders looked toward the sun. Here they could see it plainly, and it rested only a short distance above the treetops.

"So what do we do now?" Anders asked.

"I don't know," Kate answered. "But I know that God will help us." With all her heart she believed He would show them what to do.

Once more Anders started out. He changed direction slightly, then hurried on, leading the mare.

A few minutes later the trees thinned. Anders looked both ways, then walked out from the thick undergrowth.

"A road!" Kate exclaimed.

Anders grinned.

"If you hadn't changed direction—"

"I know," he said, his eyes serious. "I would have missed it."

It wasn't much of a road, but it was empty, at least for now.

"It has to go somewhere," Anders said, and swung up on Wildfire, ahead of Kate.

Once on the road, Anders slapped the reins. The black horse leaped forward. Anders dug in his heels, and Wildfire broke into a canter.

Several times Anders looked back over his shoulder. At last he slowed Wildfire to a trot. A short distance ahead of them a building appeared.

"Fish Lake School!" Kate exclaimed.

"Yah sure, you betcha!" Anders seemed awed by suddenly knowing where they were. "Now watch for the shortcut to the river."

Across from the school they found a hard-packed line of dirt into the woods. Wildfire trotted onto the narrow path willingly, as if there were water ahead.

The path led them west, then angled south. In about a mile, Kate saw blue water ahead. Logs from upstream filled the channel, but Kate breathed a sigh of relief. At least they'd come back to the St. Croix River.

"Not so fast," growled Anders. "We still have six or seven miles to the ferry. And somehow we have to cross over to Minnesota."

The tall trees on the other side of the St. Croix cast long shadows on the water. The wild river looked even more dangerous than before.

"How much time do we have?" Kate asked.

Anders shook his head. "Not much," he said. "Not much at all." As he spoke, the sun touched the top of the trees.

Anders turned Wildfire south to follow the path along the riverbank. With each bit of ground they covered, the shadows on the water lengthened.

The channel was narrower here than at Tennessee Flats. As far upstream as Kate could see, logs rode the strong current.

They had gone more than a mile when they came to a barn and a large frame house set back from the river. "Must be Powells'," Anders said.

Nearby were other buildings, and close to the water a sawmill. Along the bank next to the mill, a rowboat waited, ready for use. But Anders did not stop. With logs coming down the river, they could not use the boat.

"What are we going to do?" Kate asked. The faith she'd felt when praying already seemed far away, long ago.

Anders only shrugged.

Soon after passing the farm buildings, they came to a bend in the river. Massive logs filled the water, piled one on top of another. Some stood on end, others at crazy angles. More logs, riding the current from upstream, slammed against those already there.

Kate's stomach tightened. Crossing the wild river had been difficult enough before. Now it seemed one hundred times more impossible.

But Anders reined in Wildfire. He sat there, looking across the river. "Mighty big log jam," he said slowly.

"Hey, Anders, let's go," answered Kate. "We can't waste time."

Instead, her brother slid off the horse and walked closer to the river. When he turned back, a wide grin lit his face.

"Take a look," he said. "Take a *good* look!"

As Kate urged Wildfire forward, she felt awestruck by what she saw. Close now, she could tell how big the logs really were.

"Some of them are over thirty feet long!" exclaimed Anders. Flipped every which way, they looked like giant toothpicks.

Then Kate guessed what Anders wanted her to see. At the bend, the logs were jam-packed against the shore. "It's a bridge!" she exclaimed. "Let's go!"

The minute she spoke, Kate felt afraid. She'd heard stories about log jams—plenty of stories. Soon the men who drove the logs downstream would catch up. They'd work hard to break the jam apart. Yet even experienced men slipped off logs now and then. Every year men lost their lives that way.

Here, too, ice lined the shore. As far as she could tell, logs were jammed all the way to the Minnesota shore.

"I'm going across," Anders said.

Kate remembered Sand Creek. "If you make one wrong move—"

"I know, I know." Anders wasn't looking at her. He stared at the river, as though trying to find a path over the logs.

In that moment the sun dropped behind the trees on the opposite shore. Soon the logs that were hard enough to cross in daylight would be even more treacherous with darkness.

Quickly Anders removed Wildfire's bridle, snapped the lead rope on her halter, and led her away from the river. On the other side of some bushes, he staked her rope in a patch of grass.

Kate discovered a hollow log, and Anders pushed the bridle inside. Then they returned to the river.

"Keep an eye on Wildfire, will you?" Anders asked. "You can go to Powells'. I'll be back as soon as I find Ben."

Instead, Kate followed him down to the water. "I'm going with you."

"Aw, Kate, you've never walked on logs. It's too dangerous for a girl."

"Dangerous, you call it?" Kate lifted her head and flipped her braid over her shoulder. "Remember what Papa said? That we should stay together, no matter what?"

Anders groaned. "He didn't mean your crossing a river on logs, and you know it."

"Well, I'm not—" Kate stopped midsentence. For a moment she listened. "Was that Wildfire?"

Anders bounded onto a slab of ice. He stared back in the direction from which they'd come.

"You're right," he said, his voice low. "You're coming with me."

"What did you hear?" she whispered.

"Nothing. That's what bothers me." Anders looked uneasy. "It's quiet. Too quiet."

He turned to the river. For a moment he studied the logs again, as though seeking a path. Then he jumped off the slab of ice onto a log. It held firm.

Looking back at Kate, Anders spoke quietly. "Go exactly where I go."

With one foot he pushed down on the next log, testing it. When that log stayed in place, he hurried forward.

Kate jumped onto the first log. As she landed, she slipped. Her heart leaped into her throat. Just in time she caught herself.

Step by step Kate placed her feet carefully and moved ahead. Each time Anders went on, she followed. But then she looked down.

Water showed between the logs, looking black and cold. *What if I slip again? What if my foot drops into a hole? Worse still, what if I fall through?*

Kate froze. The terror of fighting her way out from under the logs overwhelmed her. She could not move.

"Hurry up, Kate," called Anders. "We'll soon lose our light."

Kate didn't have to be told. How much time did they have? Already the sky was gold.

"I'll watch Wildfire," she said, and the ice in her knees seemed to melt. "I'll make sure she's all right."

But Anders had already climbed to a higher log. As he looked over her head toward the Wisconsin bank, he stiffened.

"Kate," he said, his voice urgent. "There's a man coming out of the trees. He's headed this way."

Once again Kate felt overwhelmed by panic. "Can you see who it is?" Soon the darkness of night would fill the woods. Could there be anything worse than being alone with the timber swindler?

Anders shook his head. "C'mon, Kate," Anders said. "We can't take a chance on who it is."

Testing the next log, he pushed down. Again he hurried on, and Kate followed. How long would it take for the man to catch up?

As they worked their way toward the Minnesota shore, Kate looked back. Along the Wisconsin bank she saw a shadow. A shadow that separated itself from a tree, a shadow dark enough to be a man walking toward the logs.

Was it the swindler? Kate wasn't sure. She knew only that danger lay ahead. Even more danger pursued them, following from behind.

16

The Black Hat

*F*or what seemed an eternity, Kate followed Anders across the river. As if desperate to escape the shadowy figure, he bounded over the logs.

Several times Kate looked down into what could be a watery grave. Once her foot caught in a hollow. She tumbled forward, but bounced back up without injury.

A short time later, a log trembled beneath her. As it turned, she jumped to safety.

At last Anders reached the end of the jam. A narrow band of water stretched between the last log and the shore.

Anders jumped across the gap easily, but Kate was shorter. Could she make the leap?

Carefully she walked back a few logs. There she crouched and took a running jump. By just a few inches, she landed on Minnesota soil.

Without wasting a moment, Anders headed into the trees growing close to shore. Soon he found a narrow path that ran parallel with the river. Faster and faster he moved.

Is he hurrying toward Ben or from the swindler? Kate wondered. She had to run to keep up with her brother's long stride.

When they reached an opening in the trees, the large gold ball that was the sun rested just above the horizon. Anders ran on.

Finally he stopped long enough for Kate to catch her breath. "What if Ben's gone when we get there?" she asked. At that moment she couldn't think of anything worse than coming all this way and missing him.

Without answering, Anders glanced back, as though wondering if he were being followed. In the western sky, orange and red had joined the gold.

"It's sundown," Kate said. With the words she felt sick all over. "We can't possibly reach the landing in time."

"Maybe Ben will wait." Anders started running again.

Kate ran, too, and for a time she kept up. But then her head started throbbing, and her throat felt dry. Her breath rose in great gasps, and she had to slow down. Even in those few minutes the sky had changed.

"Go ahead," Kate told Anders when forced to a walk. "I'll catch up."

Her brother shook his head. "We promised Papa we'd stay together."

"That's impossible!" Kate panted still. "You're so much taller. You run faster without me."

Like a song half recalled, she thought of Papa's words. What had he told them? How did that verse go? Be strong? Don't be discouraged?

Then Kate remembered. *Do not be afraid, neither be thou dismayed: for the Lord thy God is with thee whithersoever thou goest.*

The words gave Kate strength. Even here God was with her. Drawing a long deep breath, she again hurried on.

She was stumbling, but keeping up, when a dirt trail crossed their path. The trail led down a slight hill, past some jack pine to the river.

Kate stopped and looked toward the west. In that moment the sun slipped below the horizon.

Kate turned toward the St. Croix, but Anders kept on.

"That's not the ferry landing," he said. "The landing has cables across the river."

Stretching out his long legs, Anders headed downstream. For a short time Kate followed.

Then she stopped. She wasn't sure why. She only knew there was something inside that told her to wait.

Or was it Someone? She wasn't sure. Was God trying to tell her something?

"C'mon!" Anders called.

Instead, Kate motioned to him, then started back the way they'd come. When she reached the trail that crossed their path, she ran toward the river. Rounding the jack pine, she looked down the slope to the water. A man stood on the bank.

Was it Ben? If so, he had the wrong place. In the dusk that follows the setting of the sun, Kate slowed her steps, and walked forward for a better look.

"What are you doing, Kate?" Anders called. He was catching up, but sounded impatient.

Kate motioned to him to follow.

Even from this distance, the man looked young and very tall. With slumped shoulders and back turned to them, he gazed across the river.

As Anders caught up, Kate pointed. "Do you think it's Ben?" For some reason she felt sure it was.

Together they hurried toward the man. A battered suitcase lay on the ground, as well as a bedroll. Tucked under one arm, he held a very long horn. Whoever he was, he seemed lost in thought.

As Kate and Anders drew closer, the man leaned down. He picked up his suitcase and bedroll and turned to go.

Kate stepped into his path. "Are you Bernhard?" she asked.

The young man faced her. "Yah, Bernhard Lindblom. Ben." He dropped his baggage to the ground.

As Kate gazed into Ben's face, she seemed to be looking up and up. She'd grown used to her brother's height, but Ben stood even taller—probably three or four inches over six feet.

Kate started to laugh. "You're Mama's *little* brother?"

Ben seemed to enjoy the joke. "Yah, Bernhard Lindblom, littlest brother of Ingrid," he said with his Swedish accent. His English was surprisingly good.

"I'm Kate," she answered. "Katherine O'Connell. Ingrid's daughter."

Ben offered his hand solemnly. "It is good to meet my sister's daughter."

Kate shook his hand just as solemnly. "I'm glad to meet you." Yet she felt surprised that he was not a boy but a man.

She turned. "This is my stepbrother, Anders."

"I'm glad you're still here," Anders told Ben as the two shook hands. "We almost didn't make it in time."

"Yah?" Ben's grin faded. "I would have gone away."

"We know," Kate said. "But we're here, and we want you to come home with us."

Ben looked around, as though searching for his sister. "Ingrid? She feels the same way?"

"Yah," Kate answered. "I mean, yes. She's expecting a baby, or she would have come herself."

"A baby?" Ben's smile returned.

"Any time," Kate told him. "Maybe she's born by now."

"*She?*" Anders wouldn't let it pass. "*He*, you mean."

"*She*," Kate said, in spite of Ben's presence.

Anders broke into Swedish, and Kate wasn't sure what her brother said. But Ben roared with laughter.

"You speak Swedish?" Ben asked Kate.

She shook her head. "Just a little bit. Not like Anders."

"I don't speak good English," Ben said. "I am embarr—"

"Embarrassed," Kate said.

"Embarrassed," Ben repeated. "But I speak English for you."

Kate felt moved. Already she liked this tall Swede. "How do you know such good English?"

"I work in America—" He paused, counting. "Six months I work. No greenhorn. I learn."

Kate grinned. Because immigrants sometimes didn't know what was going on, unkind people described them as greenhorns. Ben was learning, all right.

"We better get going," Anders said.

He reached for Ben's battered suitcase. "If the logs are still jammed up, we can cross the river. If they aren't, I don't know how we're going to get home."

As Ben took up his bedroll, Kate looked at his horn. It was made of wood wrapped with thin, narrow strips of birchbark. The pipe was about five feet long and had a slight bell shape on the end.

"What is it?" Kate asked.

"A *lur*," Ben told her, and the word sounded like *lure*. He seemed to think that explained everything.

"Want me to carry it?" Kate offered.

"Tack," answered Ben, and Kate knew it was the Swedish word for thanks. "I will carry," Ben added.

He held the long horn carefully, as though making sure he wouldn't bump it against something. It reminded Kate of how she felt about her reed organ.

As Anders started up the rise, Ben leaned down to pick up something Kate hadn't seen before. On his head he placed a black hat.

Kate's heart lurched. When she recovered enough to glance at Anders, she found her brother staring.

Filled with misery, Kate looked at Ben. He could have followed them. All he needed was a few minutes. The minutes when they ran ahead, then doubled back.

"Is something wrong?" Ben asked, and Kate shook her head.

Anders cleared his throat, but Kate was afraid to meet his gaze.

Anders cleared his throat again, and Kate knew he was telling her to watch.

The next instant one side of the suitcase Anders held suddenly opened. Its contents spilled out on the ground.

"Oh, I'm sorry!" exclaimed Anders. Quickly he knelt down to pick up the contents. "Forgive me, please."

But Kate knew her brother well enough to guess how he really felt. What was he doing, looking over Ben's belongings?

When he finished packing the suitcase, Anders took the bedroll instead. Walking rapidly, he led Kate and Ben up the slope near the river.

As they hurried west into the almost dark sky, they reached a place with better light. Anders missed a step, and the bedroll popped open. A neatly rolled blanket fell to the ground, along with a pair of long underwear.

Now how did Anders do that? Kate wondered. This time she had no doubt in her mind. Her brother wanted to check everything that Ben carried.

Without a word, Ben stooped down, picked up his underwear and rolled up the blanket. As he straightened up, the last bit of light reached his face.

For the first time Kate really saw Ben's blue eyes. For the first time she saw the scar on his chin.

Suddenly afraid, Kate swallowed hard. *Oh, Ben!* she almost cried out. *I want to believe you aren't the timber swindler!* Yet she couldn't push aside Joe's words. According to him, one of the strangers had a scar on his chin.

Kate glanced toward Anders and saw her brother's expression. He looked as if his eyes were glued on Ben's chin.

In the growing darkness Anders turned north and led them upstream at a rapid pace. When they reached the log jam, they found torches lit along the river.

"The log drivers are here," Anders explained. His eyes lacked the trust with which he'd first met Ben.

"Log drivers?" Ben asked, clearly not understanding.

"Men who take the logs downstream," Anders explained. He switched into rapid Swedish.

Ben nodded, but answered in broken English. "In Sweden we send logs downriver."

Out in the river several men had ridden logs from upstream. Wearing boots with sharp spikes in the sole and heel, each of them held a long pole called a pike. Its point tapered down into a two-inch thread that looked like a screw.

Using their pikes, the men grabbed hold of the logs to move them. When they wanted to unhook the pole, they gave it a half-turn backward.

Now the men moved quickly across the river, working to break up the jam. When Anders stepped onto a log close to shore, a man bounded over to stop him. "It's very dangerous," he warned.

"I know," said Anders. "But we need to get back across the river."

The driver shook his head. "If the logs let go, you'll be swept under and carried downstream. A lot of men drown that way."

"But we really need to get home," said Anders.

"Sorry," the man said. "But you can't cross now."

17

Moonlit Terror

*K*ate stepped forward. "My mother's going to have a baby. We need to get home. Can you help us?"

The log driver pushed back his battered hat and scratched his head. "Well, little lady, I don't know. She's having a baby, you say?"

Kate nodded. "Any time now."

"And you want to get home? In case she needs you?"

Again Kate nodded.

"Wait here," the man said. Turning, he ran across the logs, moving as easily as if he were on a smooth field. After talking with two other drivers, he brought them back.

"We're going to take you over," the first man said. "Once this drive gets going again, you won't get across for days. But go exactly where I show you."

Taking Kate's hand, he led her onto the logs. The torches on both sides of the river lit their way.

Whenever they came to a log standing straight up in the air, the man showed Kate an easier way around. Step by step he took her across the river.

Kate's brother and Ben came next. Behind them, the two men

followed closely in case Anders or Ben needed help.

Near the Wisconsin bank, a log moved beneath Kate's feet. She gasped and leaped quickly to the next log. Beyond that, she jumped onto shore.

"Thank you!" she called out, looking back to the driver who had helped her.

As Ben and Anders reached shore safely, the man tipped his battered hat. "Got a family myself," he said.

Then he and the other men were gone, bounding back over the logs. When they reached the middle of the river, they used their pike poles to push and pry apart the tightly jammed logs.

A minute later the logs that caused the jam broke loose. "Here we go!" called one of the men. The drivers jumped to safer positions.

Close by, a log spun beneath a driver's feet. Running in place, the man kept up with the rolling log, the way Anders had done at Wood River.

In the next instant the huge mass became a floating island. Free to move with the current, the logs swept out of the bend and down the river.

Anders started away from the water, and Ben and Kate followed. Just before they reached the trees, she looked back. A large boat was coming downstream. A square building in its center looked like a small house.

"What's that?" Kate asked.

"A wannigan. The cook-house shanty," explained Anders. He looked at Ben. "Think we ought to swim out and ask for a meal?"

"Yah, sure," said Ben. He set down his suitcase and *lur* as though meaning business.

Just talking about food made Kate's stomach growl. Ben turned to her. "You hungry?"

"We left our food in a creek," she explained. "Early this morning." It seemed days ago.

Opening his suitcase, Ben pulled out an apple. "Take," he said. "Enjoy."

Kate held the apple to her lips, ready to bite into it. Already she relished the taste in her mouth.

But Ben looked at Anders and shrugged. "Sorry. No more."

For just an instant Kate hesitated. She longed to bite into the apple, to devour every piece. Instead, she held it out to Ben. "Aren't you hungry?"

"I am hungry," Ben said. "But you are littlest." He winked sideways at Anders.

"I don't want to take your last apple," answered Kate.

"I do," Anders said. Reaching quickly, he grabbed it. But then he pulled out his knife and divided the apple three ways.

When they started off again, Kate chewed her share slowly, savoring every bite.

One minute she liked Ben and looked forward to bringing him home. The next minute she wondered, *Can I trust him?*

She couldn't get Joe's words about a scar out of her mind. Her mixed-up feelings made her uneasy.

As they left the river and the torches behind, the night grew darker. Anders headed for his horse.

In the blackness before the moon rose, Kate strained her eyes. Yet she saw no shadow, no large body, no hint of swishing tail. And she heard no welcoming whinny.

"Where's Wildfire?" asked Anders, his voice tense.

"Wildfire?" Ben wanted to know.

"My horse," Anders said shortly. "I left her here."

Kate tried to push aside her panic. "Maybe we've got the wrong place. Maybe in the dark—"

"Nope!" Her brother's voice was filled with anger. "We've got the right place."

Anders stomped around the grassy area. He peered into the surrounding bushes for any sign of what had happened.

"Maybe she pulled up her stake," Kate said, still trying to offer hope.

Anders stopped his pacing. Nervously he pounded one fist into the palm of his other hand. "It's bad enough when the swindler steals logs from the farmers. Now he's taken my horse!"

Kate and Anders and Ben searched farther out, beyond the circle of grass. Finally they had to give up.

Whoever stole the mare had left her bridle. Anders took it

from the hollow log and wrapped the long reins around his waist.

"Well, there's nothing to do but start home," he said. "It's going to be a long, long walk."

They stopped at Powells' large farmhouse, but no one knew the whereabouts of the black mare. Kate saw the pain in her brother's eyes and knew he worried about Wildfire getting hurt.

When Mrs. Powell offered supper, Anders shook his head. "Thanks," he said. "But we can't wait for you to make it. We have to keep searching."

Quickly Mrs. Powell sliced bread and cut cheese for them. Kate and the boys returned outside. In spite of her worry about Wildfire, Kate had all she could do to not swallow the food whole.

Anders moved away from the door to a lighted window. There he stood with his back to the house. As Ben drew close, the soft glow of a kerosene lamp fell on his face.

Clever, thought Kate. While Anders talked, she, too, watched Ben's face.

"We need to go on," Anders said. His voice lacked confidence, as though he trusted Ben less all the time. "Let's keep looking for Wildfire as we go. But be quiet."

Anders held a finger to his lips to be sure Ben understood. "There's a timber swindler around here somewhere. We want to find him, but not have him find us."

"Timber swindler?" Ben asked.

"A man who steals logs from the farmers who cut them. It's the same as stealing money—money the farmers really need."

Seldom, if ever, had Kate heard Anders so resentful. He switched into Swedish, as if wanting to make sure Ben understood.

Soon Ben nodded, but said only, "That's bad." The expression on his face did not change.

Ben picked up his suitcase and tucked his long horn under his arm. As they started back on the path to Fish Lake School, Kate fell in line behind her brother. Ben followed her.

Still feeling uneasy, Kate turned to Ben. "Are you used to

walking in the woods?" She spoke softly in case the swindler was nearby.

"Yah, we have woods." Ben's *w's* sounded like *v's*. "We have woods, mountains where I come from. The mountains I miss."

He lifted his horn. "That's where I use my *lur*. It is a long distance between farms. Down one mountain, up next. We talk with this."

"Talk with your horn?" Kate asked. "What do you mean?"

"I play a tune. I say, 'I'm missing a cow. Do you know where my cow is?' Someone calls back. They say, 'Yah, your cow has wandered over to my farm. I'll bring it to you.' Or they say, 'No, I don't know where your cow is.'"

"Do you have all kinds of messages?"

Ben grinned. "Yah. I say, 'Work is done. Come for party.'"

Kate smiled. "A good signal," she said.

Just then she smelled something. Standing still, she sniffed. What was it? She sniffed again, then knew.

"Anders," she whispered. "Someone's cooking meat. Do you think it's Joe?"

Anders lifted his head. "You're right! Food, food, here we come!" For a moment at least he seemed to have pushed aside his anger.

But Kate hung back. "How do you know it isn't the timber swindler?"

Anders groaned. "We don't."

"Remember what you said," Kate warned. "If the swindler stops us from talking to Big Gust, he'll get away with stealing all those logs. Just like he probably stole your horse."

Setting down the bedroll, Anders leaned against a tree. He pushed back his blond hair, as though needing to think.

In that moment a light shone through the leafless branches of a tall oak. As Kate watched, the moon rose into view. Though it wouldn't be full for another five or six days, she felt grateful for every bit of light it offered.

Still holding his horn and suitcase, Ben stood straight, alert, ready to move on a moment's notice. With watchful eyes he strained forward, listening to Kate's every word.

"How far to Grantsburg?" he asked.

Kate saw her brother's arm muscles tense. To Grantsburg? How did Ben know they were going that way?

"Have you been this way before?" Kate asked Ben.

He shrugged, as though he didn't know what she was saying.

Kate wouldn't let it pass. "How do you know we're headed for Grantsburg?"

Ben looked away, avoiding her eyes. "I came in on a train," he said finally. "I stayed at Grantsburg hotel. In the morning—"

Ben stopped, as though embarrassed to tell them.

Kate glanced toward Anders. Their gaze met. *He has to be the one Joe was talking about,* Kate thought. *How long was Ben in town?*

"In the morning I start to find my sister Ingrid," Ben said, as if he heard Kate's thoughts.

Suddenly he looked straight into Kate's eyes. "I couldn't— how you say it—work up courage?"

Kate nodded.

"I couldn't work up courage to go to the farm. I was afraid Ingrid—" Ben stopped, unable to go on.

Kate looked away. *You're so nice, Ben,* she wanted to say. Was he telling the truth? With every part of her being she wanted to believe him. She wanted to tell him, *Mama forgives you. Everything is all right.* But she couldn't speak the words.

Instead, she felt scared that she might bring home a liar and a thief. Scared that Mama would be hurt even more.

Just then Anders looked at Ben, as though wishing he could see inside the Swede's heart.

Anders is wondering too. Desperately Kate tried to recall the times she'd seen the swindler. When she did remember, she tried to push the thought away. Ben would be the same height, the same build. And there was also the black hat.

As if she'd asked Anders only minutes before, Kate recalled her words: "Can you think of anything more awful than having a brother betray you?"

A fear as cold as the ice along the river swept through her.

Anders stood up straight. "We better go."

In that moment all the times Anders had teased her fell away. All the times he had called her dumb girl no longer mattered. Instead Kate realized, *I can trust him!*

Always she had tried to keep ahead of Anders, to look better than he did. *Maybe it's more important for each of us to do whatever we do best!*

"Why don't you lead?" Anders asked her. He moved quickly, taking the place between Kate and Ben.

She started out, not liking this position any better. Yet she knew why Anders had given it to her. This way he could see what happened to her.

They had gone only a short distance when Kate heard a sound in the bushes. The next moment something dark rushed into the path. In spite of herself, Kate cried out.

Then the animal jumped up, yipping with delight.

"Lutfisk!" Laughing at her fear, Kate dropped to her knees. The dog's wet hair smelled and felt full of dirt. But Kate had never been so glad to see him.

She scratched behind his ears. Then he bounded from her to Anders.

"Your dog?" Ben asked.

"Yup!" said Anders proudly.

Lutfisk padded over to Ben, sniffed his pant legs, then backed away. Ben reached out and let the dog smell his hand.

As they hurried on, the scent of cooking meat deepened. Kate stalked forward, the hunger within her growing. She faced the moon now, and it helped her see between the trees.

Then she heard a series of hoots. The *whoo-ah!* came fourth, instead of last.

"It's Joe!" Kate whispered to Anders, hoping Ben wouldn't hear. "Did you hear that? Something's wrong."

Kate cupped her hands around her mouth and returned the warning.

When she heard no reply, she trudged on, moving as quietly as possible. Often she stopped to listen and heard no unusual sound.

But fear clutched her heart. *The swindler,* she thought. *Who is he? Where is he? Ahead or behind?*

Even with Anders walking between them, Ben was something unknown. Whose side was he on?

Moments later, Kate walked around a large jack pine. A shadow slid into the path in front of her. A shadow that had to be a person.

18

Close Call

*K*ate jumped, and the shadow moved. In the darkness of the woods she could not see the person's face.

"Be very quiet," whispered Joe. "The man I told you about was here."

"Someone stole Wildfire," said Anders. The anger was back in his voice.

"I know," Joe answered. Without a sound, he moved away, and Kate and the others followed.

As the aroma of cooking food grew stronger, Joe stopped. "I snared a couple of partridges. But the smoke and the meat might bring the man to us."

When they came into a clearing, Kate saw a small fire built in a hollowed-out place in the sand. Two forked branches stood upright, holding a third limb above the red coals. On that branch hung two roasted partridges.

Sitting close to the fire, Kate waited for her share of meat.

"It's a bit early for partridge," Joe said. "Sorry it took me longer than I thought."

"How'd you catch it?" Kate asked.

"I listened until I heard one of them drumming with its

wings. I crept up to the log he used and set my snare."

He moved quickly to give Kate and Anders a piece. But when he came to Ben, Joe paused. In the light of the fire he stared, as if seeing the scar on Ben's chin for the first time.

Only when Kate started eating did she realize how famished she was. Anders and Ben looked just as hungry. On the other side of the fire, they wolfed down the food.

While they ate, Joe stood watch around the outer rim of the clearing. One moment he looked into the trees. The next he glanced toward Ben. "Hurry," he whispered as he turned from the trees. "Every minute is danger."

"How far are we from Grantsburg?" Anders asked in a low voice.

Joe moved closer. "Eight, maybe nine miles. We stay on this side of Wood River to get back."

Kate breathed deep with relief. At least she wouldn't have to cross the ice-cold water again.

As Ben finished eating, he grinned. Kate tried to return the smile, but couldn't.

Why, he's my uncle! she thought. The idea came as a surprise, especially since Ben was only five years older than she. Even so, Kate didn't like walking through the night without knowing which side he was on.

Anders devoured his last bite and stood up. "Let's find the swindler. I'm willing to bet he has Wildfire."

"He does," Joe said in a whisper. "I came upon his tracks when I followed yours to the wild river. He led your horse away."

"He followed us right to the St. Croix?" Kate asked.

Joe knelt close to the fire. "He probably wasn't far behind. But his tracks didn't always go right behind yours."

"What do you mean?" asked Anders.

"Right after you crossed the Wood River, he followed close, along the road." Joe spoke slowly, as though choosing his words carefully. "But later on—"

He paused as though unwilling to say what he thought.

Anders prodded him. "Later on?"

Joe glanced quickly at Ben, then away. "Sometimes his tracks were in the woods, as though he stayed behind the cover of trees. Other times the tracks were off to one side of yours. It's as if he guessed where you were going and went straight there instead of following you."

"Are you saying he might have reached the St. Croix before we did?" Anders sounded tense. From across the fire his worried gaze met Kate's.

Kate looked from Anders to Ben. Her very tall uncle was listening to every word.

I'm scared, Kate thought. Again she felt divided. She had to know whether she could trust Ben. Yet she felt afraid to find out.

"How can we find the swindler without him finding us?" Kate asked.

She spoke quickly in English, hoping Ben wouldn't understand. "Anders thinks the swindler wants to stop us from talking about what he's doing."

"Anders is right," Ben answered unexpectedly.

Kate felt as if a fist squeezed her heart. Not only had Ben understood every word, he again seemed to know more than he should.

"Why do you say that?" she asked.

"When we were watching the—" Ben paused, as though searching for the word.

"The men driving logs?" prodded Kate.

"After that. The boat. You call it—" Again Ben stopped.

"A wannigan." Anders supplied the word. "A cook shanty."

"Yah, then. Man near a dark tree."

"A dark tree?" Kate felt puzzled. "Do you mean in the shadows?"

Ben nodded. "A man—how you say it?" He stood up, touched his head and held his hand out at the same height.

"As tall as you," Kate guessed.

Ben patted his flat stomach.

"Thin," Kate said out of her practice in using sign language with Tina.

Ben nodded.

Kate's nervous fingers clenched and unclenched. *Ben, you*

could be describing yourself! In that instant she felt tired all over. Tired of running, walking, worrying. Tired of crossing rivers, trying to find Ben. Tired, most of all, of wondering if he were the timber swindler.

"The man stood in the shadows, watching us?" Anders asked.

"I thought he was a—" Ben paused, then came up with a word. "A log man. But now I know he was watching you."

"What happened to him?" Anders sounded like a dog pouncing on a bone. "Do you remember anything else?"

"His hat. Black. Old." Taking off his own hat, he tapped it.

"And then?" asked Anders.

"I looked back," Ben said. "He was gone."

Anders glanced at Kate, and his mouth widened in a lopsided grin. "Just think, Kate, the swindler was probably close by all the time—just a few feet away when we looked for Wildfire! Just behind a tree when you led us through the woods!"

Trying to pretend his teasing didn't matter, Kate flipped her long braid over her shoulder. Yet she trembled, thinking how close the swindler might have been.

Ben looked solemn as he agreed with Anders. "Yah, it might be so. He looked mean." In the dying embers a shadow darkened Ben's face.

Kate glanced over her shoulder. The night sky was black now, even in the west. Like tall soldiers, the jack pine and oak surrounded the clearing, keeping watch. Yet Kate felt unable to shake the idea that a man might be standing behind a tree.

"Wherever he is, he's got my horse," Anders growled. "I want her back. And I want her back unhurt."

Moving quickly, Joe put out the fire. As the last red coal disappeared, Kate strained to see.

Far above, thousands of stars twinkled brightly. Here, where the moon shone, the ground was almost as light as day. Other places were gray, and still others completely black. The swindler could be anywhere in these unfamiliar woods.

As Kate's eyes adjusted to the darkness, she saw Anders sling Ben's bedroll onto his shoulder. Ben took up his suitcase and *lur*.

"I'll go first," Joe said.

Kate went next and behind her, Ben, then Anders. As Joe led them into the woods, Kate followed with swift, sure steps. She knew she could trust Joe's leading.

They had walked for some time when he stopped. In an opening between the trees Joe turned his head to listen.

Then Kate heard it—the sound of running water. Was Joe taking a path along the Wood River? Or a trail known only to him?

Once more he started out, and the others stayed in line. But now Kate wondered about something else. Even if they found the swindler, they had to have proof. Anders still carried the slice of wood inside his shirt. Would that be enough?

"Where's Lutfisk?" she whispered when they stopped to rest.

Anders shrugged. "I don't know. But he'll find us. I'm more worried about Wildfire."

"If Lutfisk runs into the swindler—"

"He'll bark." Anders didn't like the idea any more than Kate.

"If he'd just find the swindler, then come tell us where he is—"

But the idea seemed ridiculous, even to Kate. How could Lutfisk know he needed to be quiet? It seemed impossible. Yet the dog had so often done the right thing that sometimes he seemed human.

Before long, Joe stopped again, this time at a spring. Kate drank deeply, welcoming the coldness. Again and again each of them drank.

As they walked on, Kate again followed Joe. He moved swiftly, even in the dark, always seeming sure where he stepped.

The woods are his friend, Kate thought suddenly. In the year since moving to northwest Wisconsin she'd become comfortable with the daytime forest. But it still frightened her at night.

I think of them as my enemy, Kate realized. *Will I ever know the woods the way Joe does? Will the wilderness ever seem like my friend?*

As they continued on, the night grew colder. Kate shivered, longing for the warm coat left in the wagon. Ben opened his suitcase and gave her a sweater that hung down past her knees.

Farther on, Joe stopped again. "I'll look around," he whispered as the others drew close.

He pointed down a path that looked dim in the moonlight. "Keep going. I'll find you again." A moment later he disappeared into the night.

Kate shivered, but this time it wasn't the cold. She wished she could follow Joe. Instead, she walked on, leading the others with hands extended to feel any branch she could not see.

As they entered a stand of pines, the trees blotted out the moon. Kate shuffled her feet to feel the trail. But fear walked beside her. She tried to push that fear away, to remember her desire to make the woods her friend. Yet the darkness surrounded her, feeling as real as a person.

What if I walk right into the swindler? On that narrow trail through the pines there'd be no warning.

Kate looked back and saw only two shapes—Ben and Anders—but she felt no better. The swindler could be anywhere, just a few feet away. Around the next bush. Beyond the next tree.

In this great forest, how could they possibly find Wildfire? How could they stop the swindler so he wouldn't keep robbing the farmers? Now that they'd found Ben, Kate felt eager to return to Windy Hill Farm.

It helped her just to think about home. Then Kate remembered Mama. *What's happening to her? Maybe I have a new little sister by now.*

As clearly as if she were seeing it, Kate remembered Papa standing next to the wagon praying for her and Anders before they left.

In the next instant Kate stopped. When Ben tried to walk past her, she held out her arm. Here the pines crowded close, making it even harder to see. As Kate listened, she thought she heard running water again. Yet the night pressed in around her.

Crouching down, Kate felt the ground. On her knees she inched her way forward. Five feet beyond where she stopped, the ground fell away. Her hands reached out into air.

19

One Step Forward

$\mathcal{K}$ate's heart pounded. On her knees she moved back. "Stop!" she warned Ben.

Anders came alongside. "What's wrong?" he asked.

"I don't know." In her fright Kate's whisper sounded loud. "There's no ground left." She waited, wondering again if she heard running water.

Anders dropped to his knees and crawled forward. A few feet farther on, he lit their one remaining match.

As it flickered and went out, Kate heard Anders breathe deep. "What is it?" she whispered.

"A steep bank." His voice sounded tense, even afraid.

"A bank?" she asked.

"Cut away by high water. You almost walked into Wood River."

Crawling slowly, Kate inched back in the direction from which they'd come. When she stood up, her knees felt weak. Only a few more steps, and she'd have fallen into the rushing water. No one needed to tell her that in the dark she wouldn't have been found.

"Protection," Kate said softly. "Papa prayed for protection."

For a moment she stood there, shaken and yet moved by what had happened.

No longer did the night seem dark. No longer did the woods feel heavy with evil. Instead, Kate felt cared for by God himself.

"Well, I know one thing," Anders growled. His voice sounded worried. "If we don't all work together, nothing's going to turn out right."

"I walk in woods often," Ben said. "I will go first."

As he took the lead, his tall strong body swung through the woods as if he lived there every day. Yet it felt strange having him lead when Kate didn't know if she could trust him.

Before long, they came to the fork in the trail that Kate had missed in the dark. Soon after they started on the new path, an owl hooted. The *whoo-ah!* came fourth, instead of last.

"It's Joe's warning," Kate whispered to Anders.

When the call came again, fear knotted Kate's insides. "The swindler must be near. But where is he?"

Before long, the trail widened. Far above, the lopsided moon shone brightly, bringing a white light in the midst of darkness. Lutfisk rushed into the opening between trees.

The dog waited to have his ears scratched, then bounded away, as though wanting to show them something. Once he returned to see if they followed him. Then he disappeared again.

Not even Anders could keep up with him. It was too dangerous to call or whistle the dog back.

They had walked for some time when suddenly Anders stopped. In the stillness of the night Kate heard a whinny.

"That's Wildfire!" Anders exclaimed.

As they hurried toward the sound, the mare whinnied again. Anders left the trail. Ben and Kate followed him between clusters of young white pine. With long bluish-green needles, the thick branches grew close to the ground.

From the bottom of a hill, a light shone between the trees. A large clearing formed a semicircle, bordering the waters of Wood River.

On the near side of the clearing, two horses stood with lead ropes tied to a branch. One horse was darker than the other, and Kate felt sure it was Wildfire.

Anders hid Ben's bedroll, then crept silently down the hill. As Kate and Ben trailed behind, the carpet of pine needles deadened the sound of their steps. In the quiet they heard someone sawing wood.

Partway to the horses, Anders looked back and motioned for them to stop. Kate and Ben slid into a cluster of pines. Standing in the darkness, they looked out between the close-growing branches.

In the center of the clearing, near a great pile of logs, a farm lantern sat on the ground. Its glow fell on a man sawing the end of a log. He was big—at least as tall as Ben—and there was no doubt about the strength in his arms. The brim of a black hat hid his face.

As silent as a shadow, Anders slipped from tree to tree. When he reached the horses, he kept Wildfire between himself and the man.

While he untied the mare's rope, Anders stood close, seeming to talk in her ear. But when he started to lead her away, the other horse whinnied.

Anders stopped short.

The swindler jerked upright. Staring at the horses, he seemed to listen.

Anders stood motionless.

After a few minutes, the thief went back to work. Yet Kate could see what Anders could not. As the man drew the saw back and forth, he watched the horses.

Without making a sound, Anders led Wildfire away from the tree. When the mare's shadow separated from the other horse, the swindler put down his saw. With surprising speed, he crept toward Anders, like a hunter stalking its prey.

Suddenly Anders turned and saw the man gaining on him. With a bound Anders leaped toward his horse.

He had one leg over Wildfire's back when the swindler caught up. Grabbing Anders by the other leg, the man yanked him off and pushed him to the ground.

Anders dropped the lead rope. "*Go,* Wildfire!" he shouted.

The mare crashed through the trees, her head tilted to one side to hold the rope away from her feet. When she reached the trail, Wildfire galloped into the darkness.

With a quick movement, Ben slid his suitcase and horn beneath a low branch. Then he left Kate and the cluster of pines.

In the same moment Anders reached out and grabbed the swindler's boot. As the man tumbled to the ground, his hat fell off. Down the hill he and Anders rolled, struggling the entire way.

When they landed in the clearing, the swindler pinned Anders face down. With his greater weight and strength, he caught and held the boy's arms.

In the moonlight that shone between the trees Kate saw the swindler's face for the first time. Deep furrows lined his forehead and cheeks. Beneath bushy eyebrows, his eyes seemed cold and hard, dark with evil.

As she recognized him, Kate shivered. She had seen him before, no doubt about it. The swindler was the staring stranger!

Just then the man spotted Ben and yanked Anders to his feet. "Come any closer, and I'll hurt him!" the swindler threatened. He locked Anders in a vise-like grip.

Anders groaned and Ben froze. Then Anders kicked. His foot reached the man's leg. The swindler jumped back, but did not lose his hold. Instead, he pushed Anders toward the pile of logs.

Near the far end of the logs, the man shoved Anders to the ground and started tying him. Every few seconds the swindler glanced toward Ben.

Mama's brother stood not more than twenty feet away from the thief. As Kate moved slightly to see around Ben, her eye caught a movement in the trees beyond Anders. Who was it? Friend or enemy?

A moment later Joe stepped out from a pine on the far side of the clearing. He stood partway up the hill and behind the swindler's back.

Kate breathed deep with relief. She'd known Joe only a short time, but felt sure he would help Anders. If it came to that, she could trust Joe with her life.

But Ben? He had hurried forward to rescue Anders, then stopped, as if for her brother's safety. Even so, he and the swindler could be partners.

With every part of her being, Kate wanted to rush down into the clearing. Yet Anders had said, "If we don't work together, nothing will turn out right."

As Kate watched, Joe looked at Ben and pointed. Ben nodded slightly.

Joe motioned with his hands, as though telling Ben to walk toward the swindler, then up the hill. Barely moving his head, Ben nodded again.

Joe held up his hand, as if saying, "Wait."

Quickly Kate stepped out from the trees that sheltered her. For an instant she stood there, then slipped back within the branches.

Yet Joe had seen her. Gazing directly at the pines where Kate hid, he crossed his wrists, then pointed at Anders.

Kate caught the message. She was supposed to untie her brother. But how?

The swindler glanced toward Ben, and the tall Swede stood without moving. Behind the swindler's back, Joe knelt down. He seemed to stretch something between two trees. Then he disappeared.

As the swindler tied Anders' feet, Kate left her hiding place. Running from tree to tree, she circled around to the side of the clearing where she'd seen Joe. Silently she crept up behind the pile of logs and waited.

A few minutes later the swindler spoke to Ben. From the sound of the man's voice, Kate knew he had moved away from Anders. When she crawled around the logs, she was close to Anders, yet could see the swindler and Ben at the other end. Her uncle waited near the lantern, alert and ready for action. Without taking his gaze off Ben, the swindler picked up a gunnysack. Moving swiftly, he filled the sack with sawed ends of wood.

Staying within the shadow of the logs, Kate knelt down next

to her brother. One rope held his hands behind his back. Another rope bound his feet. A rag across his mouth kept him from speaking.

Kate worked at the rope on her brother's wrists. The knots were tightly tied, and her fingers felt clumsy with haste. Moments seemed like years before the rope slipped free.

The knot around his ankles proved even more difficult, but Kate finally loosened it. She looked at the trees behind her, then crept back, away from Anders.

From nearby came the hooting of an owl. It was Joe!

Suddenly Ben took one step forward into the light. The swindler leaped into the gap between Anders and Ben.

"Don't come any closer," the man warned again. His threat sounded ugly and unafraid.

"I don't need to," Ben said.

As he and the swindler faced each other, they seemed evenly matched. Both were tall—well over six feet, and almost the same weight. Both were solidly built.

Yet Kate saw something in Ben's eyes that she missed in the other man—a confidence, a sureness, as though Ben had no doubt that he was in the right.

In that instant Kate knew she could trust Ben. For the first time she believed in him with her whole heart.

He stood just out of reach of the swindler's long arms. When the man lunged toward him, Ben backed away, then started running.

20

New Beginning

$\mathcal{U}$p the hill Ben went, as quickly as his long legs could carry him. The swindler followed.

Anders ripped the loosened rope from his ankles and jumped up. He and Kate scrambled after Ben and the swindler.

Darting this way and that, Ben chose a twisting path between the trees. As he passed between two big pines, he slowed down a bit, as though growing tired. The man behind him picked up speed.

A moment later, Ben seemed to jump over something. In the darkness beneath the trees, the swindler followed in hot pursuit. Suddenly he pitched forward onto his face.

Joe dove from a pine tree and landed on the man's legs.

Turning quickly, Ben dropped onto the swindler's back. The man struggled, trying to throw him off. But Ben grabbed the swindler's arms, pinning them down.

"Your thieving is over, mister!" Anders exclaimed as he caught up.

The swindler had tripped on the wire Joe had stretched between trees. The big man turned his head and glared at Anders and Kate. "If you weren't around, I would have gotten away with it!"

Kate trembled and felt glad that Joe and Ben held the thief. Close up, the lines in his face seemed deeper, his eyes even more frightening.

Kate ran down to the clearing and brought back the ropes the man used to bind Anders. The three boys worked together, tying the swindler securely.

By the time they finished, a wide grin lit Anders' face. Joe and Ben clapped each other on the back, and Kate felt relieved in more ways than one. Without a doubt Ben had proved his innocence.

Yet Kate also felt puzzled. "Where's Lutfisk?" she asked. "He usually doesn't miss out on anything."

Anders whistled shrilly. A few minutes later Lutfisk padded out of the darkness. In his mouth the dog held a handle for what looked like a small sledgehammer. The heavy end dragged on the ground.

Lutfisk dropped it and sniffed along the handle. When he picked it up again, he held the handle close to the hammer and the weight balanced. Reaching Anders, the dog laid the tool at his feet.

"A stamp hammer!" Anders exclaimed. "Lutfisk must have found it someplace!"

Behind the dog came Wildfire. Anders ran toward the mare and caught her halter. With a hand on each side of her head, he looked into Wildfire's eyes. Holding out the lantern, he searched her chest and belly and legs for cuts and other injuries. Then he lifted her hooves.

Finally he patted her neck, as though unable to believe the mare was all right. Wildfire rubbed her forehead on Anders' chest.

Anders unwrapped the reins from around his waist, and slipped the bridle over Wildfire's halter. He leaped onto the mare, then helped Kate up. "How far to Grantsburg?" he asked Joe.

"Four or five miles," Joe told him. "I'll help Ben keep an eye on the swindler."

As Kate and Anders followed the winding trail to town, Lutfisk ran behind. By the time they came to the village, the first streaks of dawn lit the sky. When they reached the fire hall where Big Gust lived, they pounded on the door till they woke him.

"We've got the swindler!" Anders told the marshall.

Big Gust took one look at them, pulled on his coat, and headed toward the street. "Let's get Charlie Saunders."

Kate and Anders followed Big Gust to the red-brick house connected with the county jail. Soon the sleepy-looking sheriff opened the door.

"Got some evidence for you," Anders said, as he gave Charlie the stamp hammer and slice of wood. Quickly he told the story, ending with, "Right now Ben and Joe are holding the swindler."

The sheriff grabbed his hat, and they hurried to his livery stable. Charlie found a horse for Kate, as well as a fresh mount for Anders. They left Wildfire in the stable and saddled three extra horses. Then Anders and Kate led the men back to the others.

Along the Wood River, Big Gust and the sheriff took the timber swindler into custody. After the sheriff collected more evidence, everyone rode to Grantsburg.

As Joe started to leave, Kate turned to him. "How did you know?" she asked quietly so that Ben wouldn't hear. "How did you know that you could trust him?"

"I didn't," Joe answered. "I just knew that if you got Anders untied, we'd be at least two against two."

His dark eyes sparkled with fun. "Of course, we'd have your help, too."

Kate laughed, but then grew serious. "Thanks for everything, Joe," she said softly. "We couldn't have done it without you."

Moments later, Ben reached out and grasped Joe's hand, for now he knew the story. "I would have gone away," he said. "No sister. No Kate. No Anders."

Joe grinned. "I'll see all of you again soon." Then he was gone, running as swiftly as a deer into the new day.

Within an hour Kate and Anders finished talking with the sheriff. After a big breakfast, they came outside to find that one of Charlie's friends had brought their wagon from Tennessee Flats. Anders and Ben hitched up Wildfire, and the boys and

Kate sat together on the high spring seat. As they started home,
Lutfisk ran alongside.

On their way to Windy Hill Farm, Anders stopped to string
a new piece of wire where he'd left a single strand. Then they
hurried on, as fast as the muddy roads would allow them.

Kate felt as if she'd never been so tired, and now and then
she dozed off. Even so, the trip home seemed the longest she
could remember. As the wagon wheels turned round and round,
she wondered what was happening to Mama.

Anders broke into her thoughts. "Pretty soon we go back to
school."

"It'll be fun seeing our friends again," Kate said.

"Yup," answered her brother. "Spring term starts April 8th.
Unless, of course, we have to solve another mystery first."

He turned to Mama's brother. "Hey, Ben, why don't you go
too?"

"Me?" asked Ben. "To school?"

"Sure thing." Anders grinned. "Lots of older boys go. We
have a pretty schoolteacher. Just your age, in fact. You can sit in
the back row with me."

When Ben grinned, Anders put out his hand. "Shake on it!"

The closer they came to home, the more impatient Kate grew.
"How do you think Mama's doing?" she asked more than once.
"Do you suppose the baby's been born?"

Ben looked excited, too, but when they reached the house,
he held back. "You go first," he said.

"You come with us," Kate answered.

Ben shook his head. As though uncertain about everything,
he spoke in Swedish.

Anders translated for Kate. "He says, 'Find out if your mama
really wants to see me.' He wants to wait outside."

When Kate entered the kitchen, kettles of hot water stood on
the cookstove. Tina grabbed her around the waist and hugged
her.

"Mama?" Kate asked. "Did she have her baby?"

But Tina wouldn't tell her. Nor would Lars. He just sat at the
kitchen table, grinning from ear to ear. Then Kate saw Erik.

"Your mother's here?" Kate asked him, and he nodded.

"The baby's born?"

Erik shrugged, as though he didn't know, but Kate caught the look in his eyes. "Your father wants to tell you," he said.

"Is Mama all right?" Kate asked.

Erik smiled and said, "Yes."

Then Papa came to the door between the dining room and kitchen. "You are home!" he exclaimed. "Come, come!"

His face shone as he led Kate and Anders through the dining room toward the bedroom. Erik's mother opened the door.

Mama lay on the bed, her golden-blond hair curling around her face. The quilt was pulled high, but in the crook of her arm she held a tiny bundle.

Kate stepped forward. "Mama, are you all right?"

Mama smiled, and the glow in her eyes gave Kate the answer she wanted.

"And the baby?" asked Kate as Anders hung back.

"The baby is fine," Mama told them. "A healthy little one, I am glad to say." She turned the bundle in her arms for Kate and Anders to see.

Still Anders stayed back, as though embarrassed to come too close. But Kate leaned down for a better look.

The baby's body was tightly wrapped in a flannel blanket. Only the little face and shoulders and one small fist showed above the blanket.

The tiny eyes were closed in sleep, and thick blond hair covered the baby's head. But the face—

"It's all red!" Kate exclaimed, then wished she hadn't said it.

"Yah," said Mama, not seeming to mind. "That's the way of babies when they're born."

She turned the baby again so that Anders could see. For a long moment he stared down at the little one.

"It's really a nice boy," he said finally.

"A boy?" Kate asked. "This baby is a boy?"

"Yah, sure," answered Anders. "Can't you see his big shoulders?"

Kate stepped back, away from the bed. A rush of disappointment swept through her.

But her mother's gaze held her. "Yah," Mama said. "We have a healthy, wonderful little boy. We are grateful to God."

Kate heard the words, yet deep inside she hurt. After all these months of waiting, a boy. She swallowed against the lump in her throat.

Turning, she started toward the door, but Mama's voice called her. "Kate," she said.

Kate stopped, but did not look back.

Then Papa stood beside her. With a gentle hand he cupped Kate's chin and lifted it until she looked at him. "Mama and I want you to be the first to hold the baby."

"The first?"

"The first of all the children," he said. "Before Anders, and Lars, and Tina."

Taking her hand, Papa led Kate to the rocking chair. Carefully he picked up the tiny bundle and placed it in Kate's arms.

For a moment she wanted to give the baby back to Mama. To say, "Keep him, he's yours. Keep this little boy. I wanted a sister."

But then she looked down. Pulling aside the blanket, she gazed at the thick blond hair. It was like the down of a little chick, lying flat as she smoothed it, then springing back up.

With a nervous hand Kate opened the blanket more. Thin little legs and tiny feet, each with five toes. She counted, then looked at the hands. They were balled in fists, but each with five slender fingers.

As Kate touched one of the hands, the baby opened his eyes and looked up. He moved his head, as though trying to focus on her face.

It's like a miracle, Kate thought. *A miracle!* Her disappointment fell away.

Then she remembered the others around her. She remembered Ben, waiting to know if he was wanted.

"Your brother's here," Kate said softly to Mama. "He wants to know if you really want to see him."

"Of course," Mama said without hesitation. "Of course, I

want to see my brother. Where is he?"

When Ben came in, Kate and Anders and Papa left. It seemed like hours but was only twenty minutes before Ben returned to the kitchen.

"She wants all of you," he said.

"All of us?" Kate asked.

Ben pointed to each of them. "You and Tina. Lars and Papa. Anders too. Even me." His voice was quiet, as though hardly believing his own words.

One by one, they followed Papa back into the bedroom. Mama looked around the circle.

"Papa and I want to tell you what we decided. We want to name the baby after someone special."

Papa cleared his throat. "His name is Bernhard Carl."

Ben gasped. "Bernhard?"

Mama smiled. "After you," she said. "We'll shorten it to Bernie or Hardy when we call both of you for supper."

"For supper?" asked Ben. "You want me to stay?"

"We want you to stay," Papa said. "Yah sure, Mama and I want you to stay as long as you want."

As though unable to take it all in, Ben bit his lip, then brushed a hand across his eyes.

Mama really cares that much about Ben? thought Kate. She felt awed by the wonder of it all. *Mama cares that way, even when he hurt her so much?*

Then Mama seemed to notice Kate's silence. "Is that all right?" she asked.

Deep inside, Kate felt a glow in her heart. In her spirit the wonder grew. "It's all right," she said softly. But she meant much more.

Acknowledgments

Now and then a reader asks me, "When you write a novel, what is real?" By that they mean, "What is truth, and what is fiction?"

Perhaps the easiest way to answer is to tell you about the book you've just read.

On September 15, 1929, a fifteen-year-old girl left West Plains, Missouri. She drove a farm wagon and a horse-and-mule team. Five weeks and three days later that girl, whose name is now Gladys Peterson, reached her family's new home in northwest Wisconsin.

For most of those hundreds of miles, Gladys was alone except for a younger brother named Ellis. Ellis turned eleven during the five-week trip. Yet he and Gladys camped along the way for all but the last two nights. They overcame a number of hardships.

When I talked to Gladys, I asked, "What went wrong on your trip?"

She told me about a day when they were out in the middle of nowhere. Suddenly she looked down, and saw the iron rim coming off their wagon wheel.

To solve her problem, Gladys clipped one strand from the barbed-wire fence along the road. She unwound that wire from the other and wrapped it around the wagon wheel. The wire held the wheel together until she could reach a blacksmith!

During that long-ago trip Gladys kept a journal. I'm grateful that she shared her adventures with me. I'm thankful, too, for my young friend Shannon Benge who reminded me that when I write fiction I mix a little bit of truth with a big amount of imagination.

A number of people helped me with specific details needed for this story: Alice Biederman, Gene Blomberg and Mary Hedlund-Blomberg, Bob Gustafson, Tim Pfaff, Mildred Hedlund, Jim Hoefler, Eunice Kanne, Marita Karlish, Randy Klawitter, Floyd Lang, Lyman Lang, Jane Manders, Tom and Merle Powell, Roy and Grace Soderbeck, and Bill Young.

Others contributed to the overall content of the book and gave valuable time and suggestions while reading the final manuscript: Diane Brask, Frank and Ferne Holmes, Walter and Ella Johnson, Mary Kaliska, Bill and Alice Soderbeck, and Lolita Taylor.

Charette Barta, Ron Klug, Penelope Stokes, Terry White, Doris Holmlund, and the entire Bethany team gave editorial assistance. Still others helped in unseen and quiet ways. To each of them, and especially to Betty Coleman, Elaine Roub, and Darlene and Stan Marczak, I give my heartfelt gratitude. I am indebted also to the Grantsburg, Wisconsin, Public Library and to each of its librarians.

Each time I finish a book, I wonder what I can say about the great number of ways in which my husband Roy encourages me in this work I love. With this novel I especially cherish the laughter we shared while talking about the adventures of Kate and Anders. I hope you will enjoy that kind of fun while reading this story.